The Chronicles of Prydain
by Lloyd Alexander:

✦

The Book of Three
Taran the Assistant Pig-Keeper assembles a group of companions
to rescue the oracular pig Hen Wen from the forces of evil.

The Black Cauldron
Newbery Honor Book
The warriors of Prydain set out to find and destroy the Black
Cauldron, the Death-Lord Arawn's chief instrument of evil.

The Castle of Llyr
Princess Eilonwy is growing up and must learn to act
like a lady rather than a heroine among heroes.

Taran Wanderer
Taran faces a long and lonely search for his identity among
the hills and marshes, farmers and common people of Prydain.

The High King
Newbery Medal Winner
The final struggle between good and evil dramatically concludes
the fate of Prydain, and of Taran who wanted to be a hero.

Also available:

The Foundling and Other Tales of Prydain
by Lloyd Alexander
Eight short stories evoke the land of Prydain before
the adventures of Taran the Assistant Pig-Keeper.

The Prydain Companion
A Reference Guide to Lloyd Alexander's Prydain Chronicles
by Michael O. Tunnell

The Chronicles of Prydain

THE BLACK CAULDRON

LLOYD ALEXANDER

HENRY HOLT AND COMPANY · NEW YORK

Imprints of Macmillan
175 Fifth Avenue
New York, New York 10010
mackids.com

Printed in the United States of America by
R. R. Donnelley & Sons Company, Harrisonburg, Virginia.

Henry Holt® is a registered trademark of Henry Holt and Company, LLC. *Publishers since 1866.*
Square Fish and the Square Fish logo are trademarks of Macmillan and
are used by Henry Holt and Company under license from Macmillan.

Our books may be purchased in bulk for promotional, educational, or business use. Please
contact your local bookseller or the Macmillan Corporate and Premium Sales Department at
(800) 221-7945 ext. 5442 or by e-mail at MacmillanSpecialMarkets@macmillan.com

Library of Congress Cataloging-in-Publication Data
Alexander, Lloyd.
The black cauldron / by Lloyd Alexander.
p.   cm.—(The chronicles of Prydain; 2)
Summary: Taran, Assistant Pig-Keeper of Prydain, faces even more dangers as he seeks the
magical Black Cauldron, the chief implement of the evil powers of Arawn, lord of the Land of Death.
[1. Fantasy.]   I. Title. II. Series: Alexander, Lloyd. Chronicles of Prydain; 2.
PZ7.A3774B1 1999 [Fic]—dc21 98-40896

Originally published in the United States by Holt, Rinehart and Winston in 1965
Revised Henry Holt Edition: 1999
50th Anniversary Edition: 2015
Square Fish logo designed by Filomena Tuosto

ISBN 978-1-62779-323-0 (Henry Holt hardcover)
1 3 5 7 9 10 8 6 4 2

ISBN 978-1-250-06759-3 (Square Fish paperback)
1 3 5 7 9 10 8 6 4 2

AR: 5.2 / LEXILE: 760L

CONTENTS

Introduction to the 50th Anniversary Edition / vii
Author's Note / x

CHAPTER ONE
The Council at Caer Dallben / 5

CHAPTER TWO
The Naming of the Tasks / 17

CHAPTER THREE
Adaon / 26

CHAPTER FOUR
In the Shadow of Dark Gate / 37

CHAPTER FIVE
The Huntsmen of Annuvin / 45

CHAPTER SIX
Gwystyl / 52

CHAPTER SEVEN
Kaw / 60

CHAPTER EIGHT
A Stone in the Shoe / 70

CHAPTER NINE
The Brooch / 79

CHAPTER TEN
The Marshes of Morva / 88

CHAPTER ELEVEN
The Cottage / 95

CHAPTER TWELVE
Little Dallben / 102

CHAPTER THIRTEEN
The Plan / 110

CHAPTER FOURTEEN
The Price / 119

CHAPTER FIFTEEN
The Black Crochan / 126

CHAPTER SIXTEEN
The River / 134

CHAPTER SEVENTEEN
The Choice / 142

CHAPTER EIGHTEEN
The Loss / 152

CHAPTER NINETEEN
The War Lord / 161

CHAPTER TWENTY
The Final Price / 169

Bonus Material / 179

Introduction
to the
50th Anniversary Edition

You may have noticed by now that life is occasionally boring. Fifty years have passed since *The Black Cauldron* was first published, and in that time we humans have spent a lot of energy coming up with ingenious ways to protect ourselves from this apparently terrible state of being: television binges, social networking, 3-D movies, video games. Alongside these dazzling innovations, the ever-faithful book has jogged, year after year. I'm not going to try to convince you that any one of these anti-boredom devices is better than the others. Really, I'm not.

We ask a lot from books. We want to be entertained, to be frightened, to be enlightened, to be surprised, to gain self-knowledge, to be wholly absorbed, to feel understood, to be moved. We want one world to disappear and another to take its place. Above all we want to be *not bored*, which is something we have in common with Taran, Assistant Pig-Keeper of Caer Dallben.

We met Taran in the first installment of the Chronicles of Prydain, *The Book of Three*, when he yearned for a sword. In the opening chapters of *The Black Cauldron*, Taran is finally given one, along with a treacherous mission and a maddeningly stuck-up comrade.

Surely a sword is the antidote to boredom. Surely the

destruction of an evil cauldron that spawns undead warriors is more important than weeding the turnips or washing the pig. And if mercenary huntsmen don't keep the yawns away, there is always the small satisfaction of pushing one's horse ahead of one's rival's. Especially when that rival is outrageously smug.

Taran's instincts are wonderfully human. He wants what we all think we want: victory, in whatever form is available. As he rides toward adventure, Taran imagines a place at the table of men and, perhaps, the admiration of a certain clear-eyed princess. He wants to be good. To be brave. But he also very much wants other people to recognize his goodness. He wants both to destroy the black cauldron and to be praised for doing so. Who can blame him? It's only fair to expect praise for a hero. It's only human to imagine that a hero might not be asked to wash the pig.

When I was in fourth grade, my teacher, Ms. Tagaki, told my mother that I had an overdeveloped sense of justice. For many years, these words failed to compute. Isn't right *right*? And isn't wrong . . . wrong? And is there anything worse than having to accept—or even barely tolerate—something that is obviously and absolutely unfair?

If only Ms. Tagaki had handed me *The Black Cauldron*. This story, full of desperate sprints from terrifying creatures and dangerous arguments with powerful beings in the form of three sweetly terrifying old ladies, also delves into questions of honor and justice. There are a few folks here—the reluctant warrior Gwydion and the reluctant bard Adaon, for example—who are the personification of goodness. And there is at least one—Arawn—who is evil incarnate. But most of the people in this book, like most of us who will read it, walk the wide territory between selfless and selfish.

Taran is constantly reaching for honor and manhood, but what he finds in his grasp at the end of the story is something much more valuable: Forgiveness. Self-doubt. Acceptance. Sacrifice. With a little help from his friends (and a bit of magic), Taran is able to see the good in the seemingly evil, the weakness in the obscenely strong, the former hero in the now-corrupt warrior. He learns that there are things more important than being right. There are things more important than being brave. There are even things more important than being seen.

What Lloyd Alexander has accomplished in this short, harrowing, funny, not-for-a-moment-boring adventure is something extraordinary. *The Black Cauldron* is a truly heroic journey that ends with an unlikely embrace of our human faults, a celebration of our finer moments, and a fresh appreciation for life's less glorious offerings: a weeded garden, a comfortable horse, or a book in hand. "Is there not glory enough in living the days given to us?" Adaon asks Taran in a moment of rest between battles. "You should know there is adventure in simply being among those we love and the things we love, and beauty, too."

Rebecca Stead

Rebecca Stead
Newbery Medal–winning author

Author's Note

The following pages are intended, hopefully, to do somewhat more than continue the Chronicles of Prydain. "What happens next?" is always an urgent question, and this volume attempts to answer it, at least partially. Nevertheless, *The Black Cauldron* should stand as a chronicle in its own right. Certain matters previously hinted at are here revealed more fully; and, while extending the story, I have also tried to deepen it.

If a darker thread runs through the high spirits, it is because the happenings are of serious import not only to the Land of Prydain but to Taran, the Assistant Pig-Keeper, himself. Although an imaginary world, Prydain is essentially not too different from our real one, where humor and heartbreak, joy and sadness, are closely interwoven. The choices and decisions that face a frequently baffled Assistant Pig-Keeper are no easier than the ones we ourselves must make. Even in a fantasy realm, growing up is accomplished not without cost.

Readers venturing into this kingdom for the first time should also be warned that the landscape, at first glance, may seem like Wales, and the inhabitants may evoke heroes of ancient Welsh legend. These were the roots and inspiration. But the rest is a work of imagination, similar only in spirit, not in detail.

Readers who have already journeyed with Taran are assured— and this without giving away any surprises—that Gurgi, despite shakings and quakings and fears for his poor tender head, insisted on joining this new adventure, as did the impetuous Fflewddur Fflam and the disgruntled Doli of the Fair Folk. As for the Princess Eilonwy Daughter of Angharad—there can be no question!

I have been happy to learn that Taran, in spite of his faults, has gained some steadfast companions beyond the borders of Prydain: Beverly Bond, whose courage never faltered; Zay Borman, who rashly visited the Marshes of Morva during a thunderstorm; Carl Brandt, who was sure Prydain existed even before it was discovered; Ann Durell, from the very beginning; Max Jacobson, my severe friend and best critic; Evaline Ness of clearest vision; Louise Waller, who helped weed dandelions. And Evan and Reed, Kris and Mike, Fleur, Suzy, and Barbara, Peter, Liz, and Susie, Michael, Mark, Gary, and Diana. And their respective parents. To them, these pages are affectionately offered.

Lloyd Alexander

THE BLACK CAULDRON

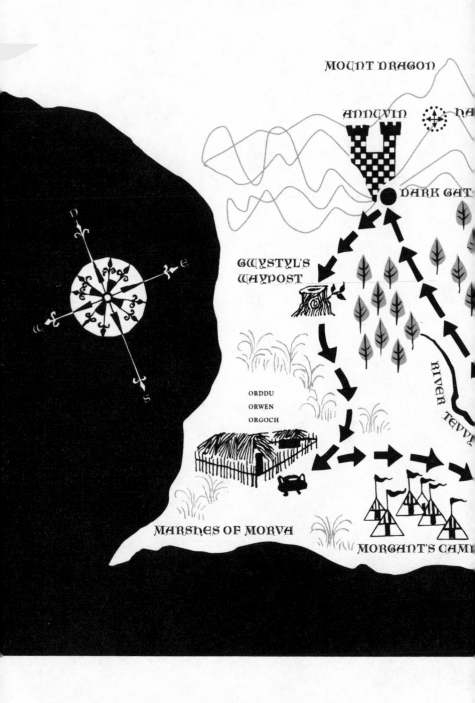

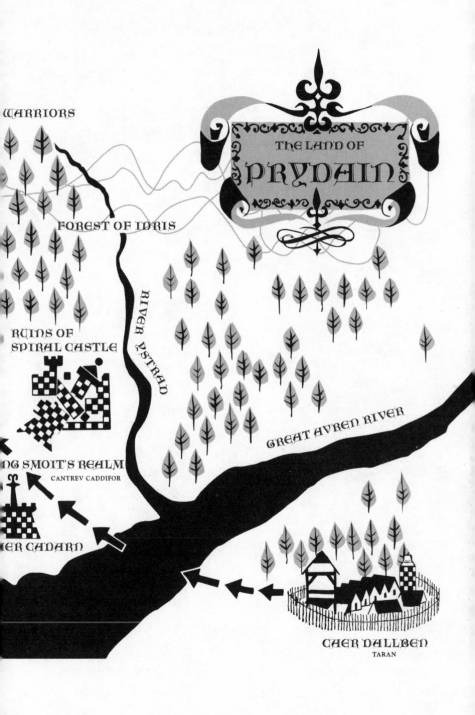

WARRIORS

THE LAND OF

PRYDAIN

FOREST OF IDRIS

RIVER YSTRAD

RUINS OF
SPIRAL CASTLE

GREAT AVREN RIVER

NG SMOIT'S REALM
CANTREV CADDIFOR

ER CADARN

CAER DALLBEN
TARAN

CHAPTER ONE

The Council at Caer Dallben

Autumn had come too swiftly. In the northernmost realms of Prydain many trees were already leafless, and among the branches clung the ragged shapes of empty nests. To the south, across the river Great Avren, the hills shielded Caer Dallben from the winds, but even here the little farm was drawing in on itself.

For Taran, the summer was ending before it had begun. That morning Dallben had given him the task of washing the oracular pig. Had the old enchanter ordered him to capture a full-grown gwythaint, Taran would gladly have set out after one of the vicious winged creatures. As it was, he filled the bucket at the well and trudged reluctantly to Hen Wen's enclosure. The white pig, usually eager for a bath, now squealed nervously and rolled on her back in the mud. Busy struggling to raise Hen Wen to her feet, Taran did not notice the horseman until he had reined up at the pen.

"You, there! Pig-boy!" The rider looking down at him was a youth only a few years older than Taran. His hair was tawny, his eyes black and deep-set in a pale, arrogant face. Though of excellent quality, his garments had seen much wear, and his cloak was purposely draped to hide his threadbare attire. The cloak itself, Taran saw, had been neatly and painstakingly mended. He sat astride a roan mare, a lean and nervous steed speckled red and yellow, with a long, narrow head, whose expression was as ill-tempered as her master's.

"You, pig-boy," he repeated, "is this Caer Dallben?"

The horseman's tone and bearing nettled Taran, but he curbed his temper and bowed courteously. "It is," he replied. "But I am not a pig-boy," he added. "I am Taran, Assistant Pig-Keeper."

"A pig is a pig," said the stranger, "and a pig-boy is a pig-boy. Run and tell your master I am here," he ordered. "Tell him that Prince Ellidyr Son of Pen-Llarcau . . ."

Hen Wen seized this opportunity to roll into another puddle. "Stop that, Hen!" Taran cried, hurrying after her.

"Leave off with that sow," Ellidyr commanded. "Did you not hear me? Do as I say, and be quick about it."

"Tell Dallben yourself!" Taran called over his shoulder, trying to keep Hen Wen from the mud. "Or wait until I've done with my own work!"

"Mind your impudence," Ellidyr answered, "or you shall have a good beating for it."

Taran flushed. Leaving Hen Wen to do as she pleased, he strode quickly to the railing and climbed over. "If I do," he answered hotly, throwing back his head and looking Ellidyr full in the face, "it will not be at *your* hands."

Ellidyr gave a scornful laugh. Before Taran could spring aside, the roan plunged forward. Ellidyr, leaning from the saddle, seized Taran by the front of the jacket. Taran flailed his arms and legs vainly. Strong as he was, he could not break free. He was pummeled and shaken until his teeth rattled. Ellidyr then urged the roan into a gallop, hauled Taran across the turf to the cottage, and there, while chickens scattered in every direction, tossed him roughly to the ground.

The commotion brought Dallben and Coll outdoors. The Princess Eilonwy hurried from the scullery, her apron flying and a cookpot still in her hand. With a cry of alarm she ran to Taran's side.

Ellidyr, without troubling to dismount, called to the white-bearded enchanter. "Are you Dallben? I have brought your pig-boy to be thrashed for his insolence."

"Tut!" said Dallben, unperturbed by Ellidyr's furious expression. "Whether he is insolent is one thing, and whether he should be thrashed is another. In either case, I need no suggestions from you."

"I am a Prince of Pen-Llarcau!" cried Ellidyr.

"Yes, yes, yes," Dallben interrupted with a wave of his brittle hand. "I am quite aware of all that and too busy to be concerned with it. Go, water your horse and your temper at the same time. You shall be called when you are wanted."

Ellidyr was about to reply, but the enchanter's stern glance made him hold his tongue. He turned the roan and urged her toward the stable.

Princess Eilonwy and the stout, baldheaded Coll, meantime, had been helping Taran pick himself up.

"You should know better, my boy, than to quarrel with strangers," said Coll good-naturedly.

"That's true enough," Eilonwy added. "Especially if they're on horseback and you're on foot."

"Next time I meet him," Taran began.

"When you meet again," said Dallben, "you, at least, shall conduct yourself with as much restraint and dignity as possible—which, I allow, may not be very great, but you shall have to make do with it. Be off, now. The Princess Eilonwy can help you to be a little more presentable than you are at the moment."

In the lowest of spirits, Taran followed the golden-haired girl to the scullery. He still smarted, more from Ellidyr's words than from the drubbing; and he was hardly pleased that Eilonwy had seen him sprawled at the feet of the arrogant Prince.

"However did it happen?" Eilonwy asked, picking up a damp cloth and applying it to Taran's face.

Taran did not answer, but glumly submitted to her care.

Before Eilonwy had finished, a hairy figure, covered with leaves and twigs, popped up at the window, and with great agility clambered over the sill.

"Woe and sadness!" the creature wailed, loping anxiously to Taran. "Gurgi sees smackings and whackings by strengthful lord! Poor, kindly master! Gurgi is sorry for him.

"But there is news!" Gurgi hurried on. "Good news! Gurgi also sees mightiest of princes riding! Yes, yes, with great gallopings on white horse with black sword, what joy!"

"What's that?" cried Taran. "Do you mean Prince Gwydion? It can't be . . ."

"It is," said a voice behind him.

Gwydion stood in the doorway.

With a shout of amazement, Taran ran forward and clasped his hand. Eilonwy threw her arms about the tall warrior, while Gurgi joyfully pounded the floor. The last time Taran had seen him, Gwydion wore the raiment of a prince of the royal House of Don. Now he was dressed simply in a hooded cloak of gray and a coarse, unadorned jacket. The black sword, Dyrnwyn, hung at his side.

"Well met, all of you," said Gwydion. "Gurgi looks as hungry as ever, Eilonwy prettier than ever. And you, Assistant Pig-Keeper," he added, his lined and weathered face breaking into a smile, "a little the worse for wear. Dallben has mentioned how you came by those bruises."

"I sought no quarrel," Taran declared.

"But one found you, nonetheless," Gwydion said. "I think that must be the way of it with you, Taran of Caer Dallben. No matter," he said, stepping back and studying Taran closely through green-flecked eyes. "Let me look at you. You have grown since last we met." Gwydion nodded his shaggy, wolf-gray head in approval. "I hope you have gained as much wisdom as height. We shall see. Now I must make ready for the council."

"Council?" Taran cried. "Dallben said nothing of a council. He did not even say you were coming here."

"The truth is," Eilonwy put in, "Dallben hasn't been saying much of anything to anybody."

"You should understand by now," said Gwydion, "that of what he knows, Dallben tells little. Yes, there is to be a council, and I have summoned others to meet us here."

"I am old enough to sit in a council of men," Taran interrupted excitedly. "I have learned much; I have fought at your side, I have . . ."

"Gently, gently," Gwydion said. "We have agreed you shall have a place. Though manhood," he added softly, with a trace of sadness, "may not be all that you believe." Gwydion put his hands on Taran's shoulders. "Meanwhile, stand ready. Your task will be given soon enough."

As Gwydion had foretold, the rest of the morning brought many new arrivals. A company of horsemen soon appeared and began to make camp in the stubble field beyond the orchard. The warriors, Taran saw, were armed for battle. His heart leaped. Surely this, too, had to do with Gwydion's council. His head spun with questions and he hurried toward the field. He had not gone halfway when he stopped short in great surprise. Two familiar figures were riding up the pathway. Taran raced to meet them.

"Fflewddur!" he called, while the bard, his beautiful harp slung over his shoulder, raised a hand in greeting. "And Doli! Is that really you?"

The crimson-haired dwarf swung down from his pony. He grinned broadly for an instant, then assumed his customary scowl. He did not, however, conceal the glint of pleasure in his round, red eyes.

"Doli!" Taran clapped the dwarf on the back. "I never thought I'd see you again. That is, really *see* you. Not after you gained the power to be invisible."

"Humph!" snorted the leather-jacketed dwarf. "Invisible! I've had all I want of that. Do you realize the effort it takes? Terrible! It makes my ears ring. And that's not the worst of it. Nobody can see you, so you get your toes stepped on, or an elbow jabbed in your eye. No, no, not for me. I can't stand it any more!"

"And you, Fflewddur," Taran cried, as the bard dismounted, "I've missed you. Do you know what the council is about? That's why you're here, isn't it? And Doli, too?"

"I know nothing about councils," muttered Doli. "King Eiddileg commanded me to come here. A special favor to Gwydion. But I can tell you right now I'd rather be back home in the realm of the Fair Folk, minding my own business."

"In my case," said the bard, "Gwydion happened to be passing through my kingdom—purely by chance, it seemed—though now I'm beginning to think it wasn't. He suggested I might enjoy stopping down at Caer Dallben. He said good old Doli was going to be there, so of course I set out immediately.

"I'd given up being a bard," Fflewddur continued, "and had settled quite happily as a king again. Really, it was only to oblige Gwydion."

At this, two strings of his harp snapped with a resounding twang. Fflewddur stopped immediately and cleared his throat. "Yes, well," he added, "the truth of it is: I was perfectly miserable. I'd have taken any excuse to get out of that damp, dismal castle for a while. A council, you say? I was hoping it might be a harvest festival and I'd be needed to provide the entertainment."

"Whatever it is," Taran said, "I'm glad you're both here."

"*I'm* not," grumbled the dwarf. "When they start talking about good old Doli this, and good old Doli that, watch out! It's for something disagreeable."

As they made their way to the cottage, Fflewddur looked around with interest. "Well, well, do I see King Smoit's banner over there? He's here at Gwydion's request, too, I've no doubt."

Just then a horseman cantered up and called to Fflewddur by name. The bard gave a cry of pleasure. "That's Adaon, son of the Chief Bard Taliesin," he told Taran. "Caer Dallben is indeed honored today!"

The rider dismounted and Fflewddur hastened to present his companions to him.

Adaon, Taran saw, was tall, with straight black hair that fell to his shoulders. Though of noble bearing, he wore the garb of an ordinary warrior, with no ornament save a curiously shaped iron brooch at his collar. His eyes were gray, strangely deep, clear as a flame, and Taran sensed that little was hidden from Adaon's thoughtful and searching glance.

"Well met, Taran of Caer Dallben and Doli of the Fair Folk," said Adaon, clasping their hands in turn. "Your names are not unknown among the bards of the north."

"Then you, too, are a bard?" asked Taran, bowing with great respect.

Adaon smiled and shook his head. "Many times my father has asked me to present myself for initiation, but I choose to wait. There is still much I hope to learn, and in my own heart I do not feel myself ready. One day, perhaps, I shall be."

Adaon turned to Fflewddur. "My father sends greetings and asks how you fare with the harp he gave you. I can see it wants repair," he added, with a friendly laugh.

"Yes," admitted Fflewddur, "I do have trouble with it now and again. I can't help, ah, adding a little color to the facts—most facts need it so badly. But every time I do," he sighed, looking at the two broken strings, "this is the result."

"Be of good cheer," said Adaon, laughing wholeheartedly. "Your gallant tales are worth all the harp strings in Prydain. And you, Taran and Doli, must promise to tell me more of your famous deeds. But first, I must find Lord Gwydion."

Taking leave of the companions, Adaon mounted and rode on ahead.

Fflewddur looked after him with affection and admiration. "It can be no small matter if Adaon is here," he said. "He is one of the bravest men I know. That and more, for he has the heart of a true bard. Someday he will surely be our greatest, you can mark my words."

"And our names are indeed known to him?" Taran asked. "And there have been songs about us?"

Fflewddur beamed. "After our battle with the Horned King—yes, I did compose a little something. A modest offering. But it's gratifying to know it has spread. As soon as I fix these wretched strings I'll be delighted to let you hear it."

Soon after midday, when all had refreshed themselves, Coll summoned them to Dallben's chamber. There, a long table had been placed, with seats on either side. Taran noticed the enchanter had even made some attempt at straightening up the disorder of ancient volumes crowding the room. *The Book of Three*, the heavy tome filled with Dallben's deepest secrets, had been set carefully at the top of a shelf. Taran glanced up at it, almost fearfully, sure that it held far more than Dallben ever chose to reveal.

The rest of the company had begun to enter when Fflewddur took Taran's arm and drew him aside as a dark-bearded warrior swept by.

"One thing you can be sure of," the bard said under his breath, "Gwydion isn't planning a harvest festival. Do you see who's here?"

The dark warrior was more richly attired than any of the company. His high-bridged nose was falconlike, his eyes heavy-lidded but keen. Only to Gwydion did he bow; then, taking a seat at the table, he cast a cool glance of appraisal on those around him.

"Who is he?" whispered Taran, not daring to stare at this proud and regal figure.

"King Morgant of Madoc," answered the bard, "the boldest war leader in Prydain, second only to Gwydion himself. He owes allegiance to the House of Don." He shook his head in admiration. "They say he once saved Gwydion's life. I believe it. I've seen that fellow in battle. All ice! Absolutely fearless! If Morgant's to have a hand in this, something interesting must be stirring. Oh, listen. It's King Smoit. You can always hear him before you can see him."

A bellow of laughter resounded beyond the chamber, and in another moment a giant, red-headed warrior rolled in at the side of Adaon. He towered above all in the chamber and his beard flamed around a face so scarred with old wounds it was impossible to tell where one began and another ended. His nose had been battered to his cheekbones; his heavy forehead was nearly lost in a fierce tangle of eyebrows; and his neck seemed as thick as Taran's waist.

"What a bear!" said Fflewddur with an affectionate chuckle. "But there's not a grain of harm in him. When the lords of the southern cantrevs rose against the Sons of Don, Smoit was one of the few who stayed loyal. His kingdom is Cantrev Cadiffor."

Smoit stopped in the middle of the chamber, threw back his cloak, and hooked his thumbs into the enormous bronze belt which strained to bursting about his middle. "Hullo, Morgant!" he roared. "So they've called you in, have they?" He sniffed ferociously. "I smell blood-letting in the wind!" He strode up to the stern war leader and fetched him a heavy clout on the shoulder.

"Have a care," said Morgant, with a lean smile that showed only the tips of his teeth, "that it will not be yours."

"Ho! Oho!" King Smoit bellowed and slapped his massive thighs. "Very good! Have a care it will not be mine! Never fear, you icicle! I have enough to spare!" He caught sight of Fflewddur. "And another old comrade!" he roared, hurrying to the bard and flinging his arms about him with such enthusiasm that Taran heard Fflewddur's ribs creak. "My pulse!" cried Smoit. "My body and bones! Give us a tune to make us merry, you butter-headed harp-scraper!"

His eye fell on Taran. "What's this, what's this?" He seized Taran with a mighty, red-furred hand. "A skinned rabbit? A plucked chicken?"

"He is Taran, Dallben's Assistant Pig-Keeper," said the bard.

"I wish he were Dallben's cook!" cried Smoit. "I've hardly lined my belly!"

Dallben began to rap for silence. Smoit strode to his place after giving Fflewddur another hug.

"There may not be any harm in him," said Taran to the bard, "but I think it's safer to have him for a friend."

All the company now gathered at the table, with Dallben and Gwydion at one end, Coll at the other. King Smoit, overflowing his chair, sat on the enchanter's left across from King Morgant. Taran squeezed in between the bard and Doli, who grumbled bitterly about the table being too high. To the right of Morgant sat Adaon, and beside him Ellidyr, whom Taran had not seen since morning.

Dallben rose and stood quietly a moment. All turned toward him. The enchanter pulled on a wisp of beard. "I am much too old to be polite," Dallben said, "and I have no intention of making a speech of welcome. Our business here is urgent and we shall get down to it immediately.

"Little more than a year ago, as some of you have good cause to remember," Dallben went on, glancing at Taran and his companions, "Arawn, Lord of Annuvin suffered grave defeat when the Horned King, his champion, was slain. For a time the power of the Land of Death was checked. But in Prydain evil is never distant.

"None of us is foolish enough to believe Arawn would accept a defeat without a challenge," Dallben continued. "I had hoped for a little more time to ponder the new threat of Annuvin. Time, alas, will not be granted. Arawn's plans have become all too clear. Of them, I ask Lord Gwydion to speak."

Gwydion rose in turn. His face was grave. "Who has not heard of the Cauldron-Born, the mute and deathless warriors who serve the Lord of Annuvin? These are the stolen bodies of the slain, steeped in Arawn's cauldron to give them life again. They emerge implacable as death itself, their humanity forgotten. Indeed, they are no longer men but weapons of murder, in thrall to Arawn forever.

"In this loathsome work," Gwydion went on, "Arawn has sought to despoil the graves and barrows of fallen warriors. Now, throughout Prydain, there have been strange disappearances, men suddenly vanishing to be seen no more; and Cauldron-Born appear where none has ever before been sighted. Arawn has not been idle. As I have now learned, his servants dare to strike down the living and bear them to Annuvin to swell the ranks of his deathless host. Thus, death begets death; evil begets evil."

Taran shuddered. Outdoors the forest burned crimson and yellow. The air was gentle as though a summer day had lingered beyond its season, but Gwydion's words chilled him like a sudden cold wind. Too well he remembered the lifeless eyes and livid faces of the Cauldron-Born, their ghastly silence and ruthless swords.

"To the meat of it!" cried Smoit. "Are we rabbits? Are we to fear those Cauldron slaves?"

"There will be meat enough for you to chew on," answered Gwydion with a grim smile. "I tell you now, none of us has ever set on a more perilous task. I ask your help, for I mean to attack Annuvin itself to seize Arawn's cauldron and destroy it."

CHAPTER TWO

The Naming of the Tasks

Taran started from his chair. The chamber was utterly silent. King Smoit, about to say something, remained open-mouthed. Only King Morgant showed no sign of amazement; he sat motionless, eyes hooded, a curious expression on his face.

"There is no other way," said Gwydion. "While the Cauldron-Born cannot be slain, we must prevent their number from growing. Between the power of Annuvin and our own strength the balance is too fine. As he gathers fresh warriors to him, Arawn reaches his hands closer to our throats. Nor do I forget the living, foully murdered and doomed to bondage even more foul.

"Until this day," Gwydion continued, "only the High King Math and a few others have known what has been in my mind. Now that you have all heard, you are free to go or stay, as it pleases you. Should you choose to return to your cantrevs, I will not deem your courage less."

"But *I* will!" shouted Smoit. "Any whey-blooded pudding-guts who fears to stand with you will have me to deal with!"

"Smoit, my friend," replied Gwydion firmly but with affection, "this is a choice to be made without persuasion from you."

No one stirred. Gwydion looked around and then nodded with

satisfaction. "You do not disappoint me," he said. "I had counted
on each of you for tasks which will be clear later."

Taran's excitement crowded out his fear of the Cauldron-Born.
It was all he could do to swallow his impatience and not ask
Gwydion, then and there, what his task would be. For once, he
wisely held his tongue. Instead, it was Fflewddur who leaped to
his feet.

"Of course!" cried the bard. "I saw the whole thing immediately!
You'll need warriors, naturally, to fetch out that disgusting cauldron. But you'll need a bard to compose the heroic chants of victory. I accept! Delighted!"

"I chose you," Gwydion said, not unkindly, "more for your sword
than for your harp."

"How's that?" asked Fflewddur. His brow wrinkled in disappoint-
ment. "Oh, I see," he added, brightening. "Yes, well, I don't deny a
certain reputation along those lines. A Fflam is always valiant! I've
slashed my way through thousands"—he glanced uneasily at the
harp—"well, ah, shall we say numerous enemies."

"I hope you will all be as eager to accomplish your tasks once
they are set out," said Gwydion, drawing a sheet of parchment from
his jacket and spreading it on the table.

"We meet at Caer Dallben not only for safety," he went on.
"Dallben is the most powerful enchanter in Prydain, and here we
are under his protection. Caer Dallben is the one place Arawn
dares not attack, but it is also the most suitable to begin our journey to Annuvin." With a finger he traced a direction northwest
from the little farm. "Great Avren is shallow at this season," he
said, "and may be crossed without difficulty. Once across, it is an
easy progress through Cantrev Cadiffor, realm of King Smoit, to

the Forest of Idris lying south of Annuvin. From there, we can go quickly to Dark Gate."

Taran caught his breath. Like all the company, he had heard of Dark Gate, the twin mountains guarding the southern approach to the Land of Death. Though not as mighty as Mount Dragon at the north of Annuvin, Dark Gate was treacherous, with its sharp crags and hidden drops.

"It is a difficult passage," Gwydion continued, "but the least guarded, as Coll Son of Collfrewr will tell you."

Coll rose to his feet. The old warrior, with his shining bald head and huge hands, looked as if he would prefer battle to discoursing in council. Nevertheless, he grinned broadly at the company and began to speak.

"We are going, as you might say, through Arawn's back door. The cauldron stands on a platform in the Hall of Warriors, which is just beyond Dark Gate, as I well remember. The entrance to the Hall is guarded, but there is a rear portal, heavily bolted. One man might open it to others if, like Doli, he could move unseen."

"I told you I wouldn't like it," Doli muttered to Taran. "This business of turning invisible! Gift? A curse! Look where it leads. Humph!" The dwarf snorted irritably but made no further protest.

"It is a bold plan," Gwydion said, "but with bold companions it can succeed. At Dark Gate, we shall divide into three bands. The first shall number Doli of the Fair Folk, Coll Son of Collfrewr, Fflewddur Fflam Son of Godo, and myself. With us will be six of King Morgant's strongest and most valiant warriors. Doli, invisible, will enter first to draw the bolts and to tell us how Arawn's guards are posted. Then we shall breach the portal and seize the cauldron.

"At the same time, on my signal, the second band of King

Morgant and his horsemen will attack Dark Gate, seemingly in great strength, to sow confusion and to draw away as many of Arawn's forces as possible."

King Morgant nodded and for the first time spoke. His voice, though ice-edged, was measured and courteous. "I rejoice that we at last decide to strike directly against Arawn. I myself would have undertaken to do so long before this, but I was bound to await the command of Lord Gwydion.

"But now I say this," continued Morgant. "While your plan is sound, the path you choose is not suitable for quick retreat should Arawn pursue you."

"There is no shorter way to Caer Dallben," Gwydion answered, "and here is where the cauldron must be brought. We must accept the risk. However, if we are too sharply pressed, we shall take refuge at Caer Cadarn, stronghold of King Smoit. To this end, I ask King Smoit to stand ready with all his warriors near the Forest of Idris."

"What?" roared Smoit. "Keep me from Annuvin?" He struck the table with his fist. "Do you leave me sucking my thumbs? Let Morgant, that black-bearded, cold-blooded, slippery-scaled pike, play rear guard!"

Morgant gave no sign of having heard Smoit's outburst.

Gwydion shook his head. "Our success depends on surprise and swift movement, not numbers. You, Smoit, must be our firm support should our plans go awry. Your task is no less important.

"The third band will await us near Dark Gate, to guard our pack animals, secure our retreat, and to serve as the need demands; they will be Adaon Son of Taliesin, Taran of Caer Dallben, and Ellidyr Son of Pen-Llarcau."

Ellidyr's voice rose quickly and angrily. "Why must I be held back? Am I no better than a pig-boy? He is untried, a green apple!"

"Untried!" Taran shouted, springing to his feet. "I have stood against the Cauldron-Born with Gwydion himself. Have you been better tried, Prince Patchcloak?"

Ellidyr's hand flew to his sword. "I am a son of Pen-Llarcau and swallow no insults from . . ."

"Silence!" commanded Gwydion. "In this venture the courage of an Assistant Pig-Keeper weighs as much as that of a prince. I warn you, Ellidyr, curb your temper or leave this council.

"And you," Gwydion added, turning to Taran, "you have repaid anger with a childish insult. I had thought better of you. Moreover, both of you shall obey Adaon in my absence."

Taran flushed and sat down. Ellidyr, too, took his place again, his face dark and brooding.

"Let us end our meeting," said Gwydion. "I shall speak with each of you later and at more length. Now I have matters to discuss with Coll. At dawn tomorrow be ready to ride for Annuvin."

As the company began leaving the chamber, Taran stepped beside Ellidyr and held out his hand. "In this task we must not be enemies."

"Speak for yourself," Ellidyr answered. "I have no wish to serve with an insolent pig-boy. I am a king's son. Whose son are you? So you have stood against the Cauldron-Born," he scoffed. "And with Gwydion? You lost no chance to make that known."

"You boast of your name," Taran replied. "I take pride in my comrades."

"Your friendship with Gwydion is no shield to me," said Ellidyr. "Let him favor you all he chooses. But hear me well, in my company you will take your own part."

"I shall take my own part," Taran said, his anger rising. "See that you take yours as boldly as you speak."

Adaon had come up beside them. "Gently, friends," he laughed. "I had thought the battle was against Arawn, not among ourselves." He spoke quietly, but his voice held a tone of command as he turned his glance from Taran to Ellidyr. "We hold each other's lives in our open hands, not in clenched fists."

Taran bowed his head. Ellidyr, drawing his mended cloak about him, stalked from the chamber without a word. As Taran was about to follow Adaon, Dallben called him back.

"You are an excellent pair of hotbloods," the enchanter remarked. "I have been trying to decide which of you is the more muddled. It is not easy," he yawned. "I shall have to meditate on it."

"Ellidyr spoke the truth," Taran said bitterly. "Whose son am I? I have no name but the one you gave me. Ellidyr is a prince—"

"Prince he may be," said Dallben, "yet perhaps not so fortunate as you. He is the youngest son of old Pen-Llarcau in the northern lands; his elder brothers have inherited what little there was of family fortune, and even that is gone. Ellidyr has only his name and his sword, though I admit he uses them both with something less than wisdom.

"However," Dallben went on, "these things have a way of righting themselves. Oh, before I forget . . ."

His robe flapping around his spindly legs, Dallben made his way to a huge chest, unlocked it with an ancient key, and raised the lid. He bent and rummaged inside. "I confess to a certain number of regrets and misgivings," he said, "which could not possibly interest you, so I shall not burden you with them. On the other hand, here is something I am sure *will* interest you. And burden you, too, for the matter of that."

Dallben straightened and turned. In his hands he held a sword.

Taran's heart leaped. He grasped the weapon eagerly, his hands trembling so that he nearly dropped it. Scabbard and hilt bore no ornament; the craftsmanship lay in its proportion and balance. Though of great age, its metal shone clear and untarnished, and its very plainness had the beauty of true nobility. Taran bowed low before Dallben and stammered thanks.

Dallben shook his head. "Whether you should thank me or not," he said, "remains to be seen. Use it wisely," he added. "I only hope you will have cause to use it not at all."

"What are its powers?" Taran asked, his eyes sparkling. "Tell me now, so that . . ."

"Its powers?" Dallben answered with a sad smile. "My dear boy, this is a bit of metal hammered into a rather unattractive shape; it could better have been a pruning hook or a plow iron. Its powers? Like all weapons, only those held by him who wields it. What yours may be, I can in no wise say.

"We shall make our farewells now," Dallben said, putting a hand on Taran's shoulder.

Taran saw, for the first time, how ancient was the enchanter's face, and how careworn.

"I prefer to see none of you before you leave," Dallben went on. "Such partings are one thing I would spare myself. Besides, later your head will be filled with other concerns and you will forget anything I might tell you. Be off and see if you can persuade the Princess Eilonwy to gird you with that sword. Now that you have it," he sighed, "I suppose you might just as well observe the formalities."

Eilonwy was putting away earthen bowls and dishes when Taran hurried into the scullery. "Look!" he cried. "Dallben gave me this!

Gird it on me—I mean, if you please. Say you will. I want you to be the one to do it."

Eilonwy turned to him in surprise. "Yes, of course," she said, blushing, "if you really . . ."

"I do!" cried Taran. "After all," he added, "you're the only girl in Caer Dallben."

"So that's it!" Eilonwy retorted. "I knew there was something wrong when you started being so polite. Very well, Taran of Caer Dallben, if that's your only reason you can go find someone else and I don't care how long it takes you, but the longer the better!" She tossed her head and began furiously drying a bowl.

"Now what's wrong?" asked Taran, puzzled. "I said, 'please,' didn't I? Do gird it on me," he urged. "I promise to tell you what happened at the council."

"I don't want to know," answered Eilonwy. "I couldn't be less interested—what happened? Oh, here, give me that thing."

Deftly she buckled the leather belt around Taran's waist. "Don't think I'm going through all the ceremonies and speeches about being brave and invincible," said Eilonwy. "To begin with, I don't think they apply to Assistant Pig-Keepers, and besides I don't know them. There," she said, stepping back. "I must admit," she added, "it does look rather well on you."

Taran drew the blade and held it aloft. "Yes," he cried, "this is a weapon for a man and a warrior!"

"Enough of that!" cried Eilonwy, stamping her foot impatiently. "What about the council?"

"We're setting out for Annuvin," Taran whispered excitedly. "At dawn. To wrest the cauldron from Arawn himself. The cauldron he uses to . . ."

"Why didn't you say so right away?" Eilonwy cried. "I won't have half enough time to get my things ready. How long will we be gone? I must ask Dallben for a sword, too. Do you think I'll need . . ."

"No, no," Taran interrupted. "You don't understand. This is a task for warriors. We can't be burdened with a girl. When I said 'we' I meant . . ."

"What?" shrieked Eilonwy. "And all this while you let me think that—Taran of Caer Dallben, you make me angrier than anyone I've ever met. Warrior indeed! I don't care if you have a hundred swords! Underneath it all you're an Assistant Pig-Keeper and if Gwydion's willing to take you, there's no reason he shouldn't take me! Oh, get out of my scullery!" With a cry, Eilonwy seized a dish.

Taran hunched his shoulders and fled, while earthenware shattered behind him.

CHAPTER THREE

Adaon

At first light the warriors made ready to depart. Taran hurriedly saddled the gray, silver-maned Melynlas, colt of Gwydion's own steed Melyngar. Gurgi, miserable as a wet owl at being left behind, helped load the saddlebags. Dallben had changed his mind about not seeing anyone and stood silent and thoughtful in the cottage doorway, with Eilonwy beside him.

"I'm not speaking to you!" she cried to Taran. "The way you acted. That's like asking someone to a feast, then making them wash the dishes! But—farewell, anyway. That," she added, "doesn't count as speaking."

Gwydion leading, the horsemen moved through the swirling mist. Taran rose in his saddle, turned, and waved proudly. The white cottage and the three figures grew smaller. Field and orchard fell away, as Melynlas cantered into the trees. The forest closed behind Taran and he could see Caer Dallben no more.

With a whinny of alarm, Melynlas suddenly reared. As Ellidyr had ridden up behind Taran, his steed had reached out her long neck and given the stallion a spiteful nip. Taran clutched at the reins and nearly fell.

"Keep your distance from Islimach," said Ellidyr with a raw laugh. "She bites. We are much alike, Islimach and I."

Taran was about to reply angrily when Adaon, who had seen what happened, drew his bay mare to Ellidyr's side. "You are right, Son of Pen-Llarcau," Adaon said. "Your horse carries a difficult burden. And so do you."

"What burden do I carry?" cried Ellidyr, bristling.

"Last night I dreamed of us all," Adaon said, thoughtfully fingering the iron clasp at his throat. "You I saw with a black beast on your shoulders. Beware, Ellidyr, lest it swallow you up," he added, the gentleness of his tone softening the harshness of his counsel.

"Spare me from pig-boys and dreamers!" Ellidyr retorted, and with a shout urged Islimach farther up the column.

"And I?" Taran asked. "What did your dream tell of me?"

"You," answered Adaon, after a moment's hesitation, "you were filled with grief."

"What cause have I to grieve?" asked Taran, surprised. "I am proud to serve Lord Gwydion, and there is a chance to win much honor, more than by washing pigs and weeding gardens!"

"I have marched in many a battle host," Adaon answered quietly, "but I have also planted seeds and reaped the harvest with my own hands. And I have learned there is greater honor in a field well plowed than in a field steeped in blood."

The column had begun to move more rapidly and they quickened their steeds' gaits. Adaon rode easily and skillfully; head high, an open smile on his face, he seemed to be drinking in the sights and sounds of the morning. While Fflewddur, Doli, and Coll kept pace with Gwydion, and Ellidyr followed sullenly behind King Morgant's troop, Taran kept to Adaon's side along the leaf-strewn path.

As they spoke together to ease the rigors of their journey, Taran soon realized there was little Adaon had not seen or done. He had sailed far beyond the Isle of Mona, even to the northern sea; he had worked at the potter's wheel, cast nets with the fisherfolk, woven cloth at the looms of the cottagers; and, like Taran, labored over the glowing forge. Of forest lore he had studied deeply, and Taran listened in wonder as Adaon told the ways and natures of woodland creatures, of bold badgers and cautious dormice and geese winging under the moon.

"There is much to be known," said Adaon, "and above all much to be loved, be it the turn of the seasons or the shape of a river pebble. Indeed, the more we find to love, the more we add to the measure of our hearts."

Adaon's face was bright in the early rays of the sun, but a trace of longing had come into his voice. When Taran asked him what was amiss, he did not answer immediately, as though he wished to hold his own thoughts.

"My heart will be lighter when our task is done," Adaon said at last. "Arianllyn, my betrothed, waits for me in the northern domains, and the sooner Arawn's cauldron is destroyed, the sooner may I return to her."

By day's end, they had become fast friends. At nightfall, when Taran rejoined Gwydion and his companions, Adaon camped with them. They had already crossed Great Avren and were well on their way to the borders of King Smoit's realm. Gwydion was satisfied with their progress, though he warned them the most difficult and dangerous portion of their journey was to come.

All were in good spirits save Doli, who hated riding horseback and gruffly declared he could go faster afoot. As the companions rested in a protected grove, Fflewddur offered his harp to Adaon and urged him to play. Adaon, sitting comfortably with his back against a tree, put the instrument to his shoulder. For a moment he was thoughtful, his head bowed, then his hands gently touched the strings.

The voice of the harp and Adaon's voice twined one with the other in harmonies Taran never before had heard. The tall man's face was raised toward the stars and his gray eyes seemed to see far beyond them. The forest had fallen silent; the night sounds were stilled.

The song of Adaon was not a warrior's lay but one of peacefulness and deep joy, and as Taran listened, its echoes rang again and again in his heart. He longed for the music to continue, but Adaon stopped, almost abruptly, and with a grave smile handed the harp back to Fflewddur.

The companions wrapped themselves in their cloaks and slept. Ellidyr remained aloof from them, stretched on the ground at the hooves of his roan. Taran, his head pillowed on his saddle, his hand on his new sword, was impatient for dawn and eager to resume the journey. Yet, as he dropped into slumber, he recalled Adaon's dream and felt a shadow like the flutter of a dark wing.

Next day the companions crossed the River Ystrad and began bearing northward. With much loud grumbling at being kept from the quest, King Smoit obeyed Gwydion and turned away from the column, riding toward Caer Cadarn to ready his warriors. Later, the pace of the column slowed as the pleasant meadows wrinkled into hills. Shortly after midday the horsemen entered the Forest of Idris. Here, the brown, withered grasses were sharp as thorns. Once familiar oaks and alders appeared strange to Taran; their dead leaves clung to the tangled branches and the black trunks jutted like charred bones.

At length the forest broke away to reveal sheer faces of jagged

cliffs. Gwydion signaled the company forward. Taran's throat tightened. For a cold instant he shrank from urging Melynlas up the
stony slope. He knew, without a word from Gwydion, that the Dark
Gate of Annuvin was not far distant.

Narrow trails rising above deep gorges now forced the company
to go in single file. Taran, Adaon, and Ellidyr had been jogging at
the end of the column, but Ellidyr kicked his heels against
Islimach's flanks and thrust his way past Taran.

"Your place is at the rear, pig-boy!" he called.

"And your place is where you earn it," cried Taran, giving
Melynlas rein to strive ahead.

The horses jostled; the riders struggled knee against knee.
Islimach reared and neighed wildly. With his free hand Ellidyr
seized the bridle of Melynlas to force the stallion back. Taran tried
to turn his mount's head but Melynlas, in a shower of pebbles,
slipped from the trail to the steep slope. Taran, flung out of the saddle, clutched at the rocks to break his fall.

Melynlas, more surefooted than his master, regained his balance
on a ledge below the trail. Taran, sprawled flat against the stones,
tried vainly to clamber back to the path. Adaon dismounted
instantly, ran to the edge of the slope, and attempted to grasp
Taran's hands. Ellidyr, too, dismounted. He brushed Adaon aside,
leaped down, and seized Taran under the arms. With a powerful
heave, he lofted Taran like a sack of meal to the safety of the trail.
Picking his way toward Melynlas, Ellidyr put his shoulder beneath
the saddle girth and strained mightily. With all his strength, little
by little, he raised Melynlas until the stallion was able to clamber
from the ledge.

"You fool!" Taran threw back at Ellidyr, racing to Melynlas and anxiously examining the steed. "Has your pride crowded all the wits out of your head?" Melynlas, he saw with relief, was unharmed. Despite himself, he glanced at Ellidyr in amazement and not without a certain admiration. "I have never seen such a feat of strength," Taran admitted.

Ellidyr, for the first time, seemed confused and frightened. "I did not mean for you to fall," he began. Then he threw back his head and, with a mocking smile, added, "My concern is for your steed, not your skin."

"I, too, admire your strength, Ellidyr," Adaon said sharply. "But it is to your shame you proved it thus. The black beast rides in the saddle with you. I see it even now."

One of Morgant's warriors, hearing the clamor, had given the alarm. A moment later Gwydion, followed by King Morgant, strode back along the trail. Behind them hurried the agitated Fflewddur and the dwarf.

"Your pig-boy had no better sense than to force his way ahead of me," Ellidyr said to Gwydion. "Had I not pulled him and his steed back . . ."

"Is this true?" Gwydion asked, glancing at Taran and his torn clothing.

Taran, about to answer, shut his lips tightly and nodded his head. He saw the look of surprise on Ellidyr's angry face.

"We have no lives to waste," Gwydion said, "yet you have risked two. I cannot spare a man or I would send you back to Caer Dallben this instant. But I shall, if this happens again. And you, too, Ellidyr, or any of this company."

King Morgant stepped forward. "This proves what I had feared, Lord Gwydion. Our way is difficult, even unburdened with the cauldron. Once we gain it, I urge you again not to return to Caer Dallben. It would be wiser to take the cauldron north, into my realm.

"I think, too," Morgant continued, "that a number of my own warriors should be dispatched to guard our retreat. In exchange I offer these three," he said, gesturing toward Taran, Adaon, and Ellidyr, "a place among my horsemen when I attack. If I read their faces well, they would prefer it to waiting in reserve."

"Yes!" cried Taran, gripping his sword. "Let us join the attack!"

Gwydion shook his head. "The plan shall be as I set it. Mount quickly, we have already lost much time."

King Morgant's eyes flickered. "It shall be as you command, Lord Gwydion."

"What happened?" whispered Fflewddur to Taran. "Don't tell me Ellidyr wasn't to blame somehow. He's a troublemaker, I can see it. I can't imagine what Gwydion was thinking of when he brought him along."

"The blame is as much mine," said Taran. "I behaved no better than he did. I should have held my tongue. With Ellidyr," he added, "that's not easy to do."

"Yes," the bard sighed, glancing at his harp. "I have a rather similar difficulty."

Throughout the next day the company went with greatest caution, for flights of gwythaints, Arawn's fearsome messenger birds, were now seen against the clouds. Shortly before dusk, the trail led downward toward a shallow basin set with scrub and pines. There, Gwydion halted. Ahead rose the baleful crags of Dark Gate, its twin slopes blazing crimson in the dying sun.

Thus far the company had encountered no Cauldron-Born. Taran deemed this lucky, but Gwydion frowned uneasily.

"I fear the Cauldron-Born more when they cannot be seen," Gwydion said, after calling the warriors around him. "I would almost believe they had deserted Annuvin. But Doli brings news I wish I might spare you."

"Had me turn invisible and run ahead, that's what he did," Doli furiously muttered to Taran. "When we go into Annuvin, I'll have to do it again. Humph! My ears already feel like a swarm of bees!"

"Take heed, all of you," Gwydion went on. "The Huntsmen of Annuvin are abroad."

"I have faced the Cauldron-Born," Taran boldly cried. "These warriors can be no more terrible."

"Do you believe so?" Gwydion replied with a grim smile. "I dread them as much. They are ruthless as the Cauldron-Born, their strength even greater. They go afoot, yet they are swift, with much endurance. Fatigue, hunger, and thirst mean little to them."

"The Cauldron-Born are deathless," Taran said. "If these are mortal men, they can be slain."

"They are mortal," Gwydion answered, "though I scorn to call them men. They are the basest of warriors who have betrayed their comrades; murderers who have killed for the joy of it. To indulge their own cruelty they have willingly chosen Arawn's realm and have sworn allegiance to him with a blood oath even they cannot break.

"Yes," Gwydion added, "they can be slain. But Arawn has forged them into a brotherhood of killers and given them a terrible power. They rove in small bands, and within those companies the death of one man only adds to the strength of all the rest.

"Shun them," Gwydion warned. "Do not give battle if it is possible to avoid it. For the more you strike down, the more the others gain in strength. Even as their number dwindles, their power grows.

"Conceal yourselves now," he ordered, "and sleep. Our attack must be tonight."

Restless, Taran could barely force himself to close his eyes. When he did, it was in light, uneasy slumber. He woke with a start, groping for his sword. Adaon, already awake, cautioned him to silence. The moon rode high, cold and glittering. The warriors of King Morgant's train moved like shadows. There was a faint jingle of harness, the whisper of a blade drawn from its sheath.

Doli, having turned himself invisible, had departed toward Dark Gate. Taran found the bard strapping his beloved harp more securely to his shoulders. "I doubt I'll really need it," Fflewddur admitted. "On the other hand, you never know what you'll be called on to do. A Fflam is always prepared!"

Beside him, Coll had just donned a close-fitting, conical helmet. The sight of the stouthearted old warrior, and the cap hardly seeming enough to protect his bald head, filled Taran suddenly with sadness. He threw his arms around Coll and wished him good fortune.

"Well, my boy," said Coll, winking, "never fear. We'll be back before you know it. Then, off to Caer Dallben and the task is done."

King Morgant, cloaked heavily in black, halted at Taran's side. "It would have done me honor to count you among my men," he said. "Gwydion has told me a little of you, and I have seen you for myself. I am a warrior and recognize good mettle."

This was the first time Morgant had ever spoken directly to him, and Taran was so taken aback with surprise and pleasure that he could not even stammer out an answer before the war-leader strode away to his horse.

Taran caught sight of Gwydion astride Melyngar and ran to him. "Let me go with you," he pleaded again. "If I was man enough to sit with you in council and to come this far, I am man enough to ride with your warriors."

"Do you love danger so much?" asked Gwydion. "Before you are a man," he added gently, "you will learn to hate it. Yes, and fear it, too, even as I do." He reached down and clasped Taran's hand. "Keep a bold heart. Your courage will be tested enough."

Disappointed, Taran turned away. The riders vanished beyond the trees and the grove seemed empty and desolate. Melynlas, teth-ered among the other steeds, whinnied plaintively.

"This night will be long," Adaon said, looking intently past the shadows at the brooding heights of Dark Gate. "You, Taran, shall stand first watch; Ellidyr second, until the moon is down."

"So you shall have more time for dreaming," Ellidyr said with a scornful laugh.

"You will find no quarrel with my dreams tonight," replied Adaon good-naturedly, "for I will share the watch with both of you. Sleep, Ellidyr," he added, "or if you will not sleep, at least keep silent."

Ellidyr angrily wrapped himself in his cloak and threw himself on the ground near Islimach. The roan whickered and bent her neck, nuzzling her master.

The night was chill. Frost had begun to sparkle on the dry sedge and a cloud trailed across the moon. Adaon drew his sword and stepped to the edge of the trees. The white light caught his eyes, turning them brilliant as starshine. He was silent, head raised, alert as a wild creature of the forest.

"Do you think they've gone into Annuvin yet?" Taran whispered.

"They should soon be there," Adaon answered.

"I wish Gwydion had let me go with him," Taran said with a certain bitterness. "Or with Morgant."

"Do not wish that," Adaon said quickly. His face held a look of concern.

"Why not?" asked Taran, puzzled. "I would have been proud to follow Morgant. Next to Gwydion, he is the greatest war lord in Prydain."

"He is a brave and powerful man," Adaon agreed, "but I am uneasy for him. In my dream, the night before we left, warriors rode a slow circle around him and Morgant's sword was broken and weeping blood."

"Perhaps there is no meaning in it," Taran suggested, as much to reassure himself as Adaon. "Does it always happen—that your dreams are always true?"

Adaon smiled. "There is truth in all things, if you understand them well."

"You never told me what you dreamed of the others," Taran said. "Of Coll or good old Doli—or yourself, for the matter of that."

Adaon did not reply, but turned again and looked toward Dark Gate.

Unsheathing his sword, Taran moved worriedly to the edge of the grove.

CHAPTER FOUR

In the Shadow of Dark Gate

The night passed heavily, and it was nearly time for Ellidyr's turn at guard, when Taran heard a rustling in the shrub. He raised his head abruptly. The sound stopped. He was unsure now that he had really heard it. He held his breath and waited, poised and tense.

Adaon, whose ears were as keen as his eyes, had also noticed it and was at Taran's side in an instant.

There was, it seemed to Taran, a flicker of light. A branch cracked nearby. With a shout, Taran swung up his blade and leaped toward it. A golden beam flashed in his eyes and a squeal of indignation struck his ears.

"Put down that sword!" Eilonwy cried. "Every time I see you, you're waving it around or pointing it at somebody."

Taran fell back dumbfounded. As he did, a dark figure bounded past Ellidyr, who sprang to his feet, his blade unsheathed and whistling through the air.

"Help! Help!" howled Gurgi. "Angry lord will harm Gurgi's poor tender head with slashings and gashings!" He scuttled halfway up a pine tree, and from the safety of his perch shook a fist at the astonished Ellidyr.

Taran pulled Eilonwy into the protection of the grove. Her hair was disheveled, her robe torn and mud-stained. "What have you done?" he cried. "Do you want us all killed? Put out that light!" He seized the glowing sphere and fumbled vainly with it.

"Oh, you'll never learn how to use my bauble," Eilonwy said with impatience. She took back the golden ball, cupped it in her hand, and the light vanished.

Adaon, recognizing the girl, put his hand anxiously on her shoulder. "Princess, Princess, you should not have followed us."

"Of course she shouldn't," Taran put in angrily. "She must return immediately. She's a foolish, scatterbrained . . ."

"She is uncalled and unwanted here," said Ellidyr, striding up. He turned to Adaon. "For once the pig-boy shows sense. Send the little fool back to her pots."

Taran spun around. "Hold your tongue! I have swallowed your insults to me for the sake of our quest, but you will not speak ill of another."

Ellidyr's sword leaped up. Taran raised his own. Adaon stepped between them and held out his hands. "Enough, enough," he ordered. "Are you so eager to shed blood?"

"Must I hear reproof from a pig-boy?" retorted Ellidyr. "Must I let a scullery maid cost me my head?"

"Scullery maid!" shrieked Eilonwy. "Well, I can tell you . . ."

Gurgi, meantime, had clambered cautiously from the tree and had loped over to stand behind Taran.

"And this!" Ellidyr laughed bitterly, gesturing at Gurgi. "This— thing! Is this the black beast that so alarmed you, dreamer?"

"No, Ellidyr, it is not," murmured Adaon, almost sadly.

"This is Gurgi the warrior!" Gurgi boldly cried over Taran's shoulder. "Yes, yes! Clever, valiant Gurgi, who joins master to keep him from harmful hurtings!"

"Be silent," Taran ordered. "You've caused trouble enough."

"How did you reach us?" Adaon asked. "You are on foot."

"Well, not really," Eilonwy said, "at least, not all the way. The horses didn't run off until a little while ago."

"What?" cried Taran. "You took horses from Caer Dallben and lost them?"

"You know perfectly well they're our own horses," declared Eilonwy, "the ones Gwydion gave us last year. And we didn't lose them. It was more as if they lost us. We only stopped to let them drink and the silly things galloped away. Frightened, I suppose. I think they didn't like being so close to Annuvin, though I'll tell you truthfully it doesn't bother me in the least.

"In any case," she concluded, "you needn't worry about them. The last we saw, they were heading straight for Caer Dallben."

"And so shall you be," Taran said.

"And so shall I not!" cried Eilonwy. "I thought about it a long time after you left, every bit as long as it took you to cross the fields. And I decided. It doesn't matter what anybody says, fair is fair. If you can be allowed on a quest, so can I. And there it is, as simple as that."

"And it was clever Gurgi who found the way!" Gurgi put in proudly. "Yes, yes, with whiffings and sniffings! Gurgi does not let gentle Princess go alone, oh, no! And loyal Gurgi does not leave friends behind," he added reproachfully to Taran.

"Since you have come this far," Adaon said, "you may await Gwydion. Although how he will deal with you two runaways may not be to your liking. Your journey," he added, smiling at the bedraggled Princess, "seems to have been more difficult than ours. Rest now and take refreshment."

"Yes, yes!" Gurgi cried. "Crunchings and munchings for brave, hungry Gurgi!"

"That's very kind and thoughtful of you," said Eilonwy with an admiring glance at Adaon. "Much more than you can expect from certain Assistant Pig-Keepers."

Adaon went to the stock of provisions, while Ellidyr strode off to his guard post. Taran sat down wearily on a boulder, his sword across his knees.

"It's not that we're starving," Eilonwy said. "Gurgi did remember to bring along the wallet of food. Yes, and that was a gift from Gwydion, too, so he had every right to take it. It's certainly a magical wallet," she went on; "it never seems to get empty. The food is really quite nourishing, I'm sure, and wonderful to have when you need it. But the truth of the matter is, it's rather tasteless. That's often the trouble with magical things. They're never quite what you'd expect.

"You're angry, aren't you," Eilonwy went on. "I can always tell. You look as if you've swallowed a wasp."

"If you'd stopped to think of the danger," Taran replied, "instead of rushing off without knowing what you're doing."

"You're a fine one to talk, Taran of Caer Dallben," said Eilonwy. "Besides, I don't think you're as angry as all that, not after what you said to Ellidyr. It was wonderful the way you were ready to smite him because of me. Not that you needed to. I could have taken good care of him myself. And I didn't mean you weren't kind and thoughtful. You really are. It just doesn't always occur to you. For an Assistant Pig-Keeper you do amazingly well . . ."

Before Eilonwy could finish, Ellidyr gave a shout of warning. A horse and rider plunged into the grove. It was Fflewddur. Behind him galloped Doli's shaggy pony.

Breathless, and with his yellow hair pointing in all directions, the bard flung himself from the steed and ran to Adaon. "Make ready to leave!" he cried. "Take the weapons. Get the pack horses moving. We're going to Caer Cadarn . . ." He caught sight of Eilonwy. "Great Belin! What are you doing here?"

"I'm tired of being asked that," Eilonwy said.

"The cauldron!" cried Taran. "Did you seize it? Where are the others? Where is Doli?"

"Here, where else?" snapped a voice. In another instant Doli flickered into sight astride what had seemed to be an empty saddle. He jumped heavily to the ground. "Didn't even take time to make myself visible again." He clapped his hands to his head. "Oh, my ears!"

"Gwydion orders us to fall back immediately," the bard went on in great excitement. "He and Coll are with Morgant. They'll catch us up if they can. If not, we all rally at Caer Cadarn."

While Ellidyr and Adaon hurriedly untethered the animals, Taran and the bard packed the store of weapons. "Keep these," Fflewddur ordered, pressing a bow and quiver of arrows into Eilonwy's hands. "And the rest of you, arm yourselves well."

"What happened?" Taran asked fearfully. "Did the plan fail?"

"The plan?" Fflewddur asked. "That was perfect. Couldn't have been better. Morgant and his men rode with us to Dark Gate—ah, that Morgant! What a warrior! Not a nerve in him. Cool as you please. You might have thought he was going to a feast." The bard shook his spiky head. "And there we were, on the very threshold of Annuvin! Oh, you'll hear songs about that, mark my words."

"Stop yammering," ordered Doli, hastening up with the agitated pack horses. "Yes, the *plan* was fine," he cried angrily. "It would have gone slick as butter. There was only one thing wrong. We wasted our time and risked our necks for nothing!"

"Will one or the other of you make sense?" Eilonwy burst out. "I don't care about songs or butter! Tell us straight out! Where is the cauldron?"

"I don't know," said the bard. "Nobody knows."

"You didn't lose it!" Eilonwy gasped, clapping a hand to her mouth. "No! Oh, you pack of ninnies! Great heroes! I knew I should have gone with you from the beginning."

Doli looked as if he were about to explode. His ears trembled; he raised himself on tiptoe, his fists clenched. "Don't you understand? The cauldron is gone! Away! Not there!"

"That's not possible!" Taran cried.

"Don't tell me it isn't possible," Doli snapped. "I was there. I know what I saw. I know what I heard. I went in first, just as Gwydion ordered. I found the Hall of Warriors. No trouble at all. No guards, in fact. Aha, think I, this will be easier than whistling. I slipped in—I could have done it in full view in broad daylight. And why? Because there's nothing to guard! The platform was empty!"

"Arawn has moved the cauldron," Taran interrupted. "There is a new hiding place; he's locked it up somewhere else."

"Don't you think I have the wits I was born with?" Doli retorted. "That was the first thing that came into my head. So I set off again—I'd have searched Arawn's own chamber if I'd had to. But I hadn't gone six paces before I ran into a pair of Arawn's guards. Or they ran into me, the clumsy oafs," Doli muttered, rubbing a bruised eye. "I went along with them a little way. By then, I'd heard enough.

"It must have happened a few days ago. How or who, I don't know. Neither does Arawn. You can imagine his rage! But whoever they were, they got there ahead of us. They did their work well. The cauldron is gone from Annuvin!"

"But that's wonderful!" said Eilonwy. "Our task is done and it cost us nothing more than a journey."

"Our task is far from done," said the grave voice of Adaon. He had finished loading one of the pack horses and had come to stand beside Taran. Ellidyr, too, had been listening closely.

"We've lost the glory of fighting for it," Taran said. "But the important thing is that Arawn has it no longer."

"It is not so easy," Adaon warned. "This is a stinging defeat for Arawn; he will do all in his power to regain the cauldron. But there is more. The cauldron is dangerous in itself, even out of Arawn's grasp. What if it has fallen into other evil hands?"

"Exactly what Gwydion himself said," Fflewddur put in. "The thing has somehow got to be found and destroyed without delay. Gwydion will plan a new search from Caer Cadarn. It would seem our work has just begun."

"Mount your steeds," Adaon ordered. "We cannot overburden our pack animals; the Princess Eilonwy and Gurgi will share our own horses."

"Islimach will bear only me," Ellidyr said. "She has been trained so, from a foal."

"I would expect that, being a steed of yours," Taran said. "Eilonwy will ride with me."

"And I shall take Gurgi with me on Lluagor," Adaon said. "Come now, quickly."

Taran ran to Melynlas, leaped astride, and pulled Eilonwy up after him. Doli and the others hastened to mount. But as they did, savage cries burst from either side of them and there was a sudden hiss of arrows.

CHAPTER FIVE

The Huntsmen of Annuvin

The pack horses shrieked in terror. Melynlas reared, as arrows rattled among the branches. Fflewddur, sword in hand, spun his mount and plunged against the attackers.

Adaon's voice rang above the din. "These are Huntsmen! Fight free of them!"

At first it seemed to Taran the shadows had sprung to life. Formless, they drove against him, seeking to tear him from his saddle. He swung his sword blindly. Melynlas pitched furiously, trying to break away from the press of warriors.

The sky had begun to unravel in scarlet threads. The sun, rising against black pines and leafless trees, filled the grove with a baleful light.

Taran now saw the attackers numbered about a dozen. They wore jackets and leggings of animal skins. Long knives were thrust into their belts, and from the neck of one warrior hung a curved hunting horn. As the men swirled around him, Taran caught his breath in horror. Each Huntsman bore a crimson brand on his forehead. The sight of it filled Taran with dread, for he knew the strange symbol must be a mark of Arawn's power. He fought against the fear that chilled his heart and drained his strength.

Behind him, he heard Eilonwy cry out. Then he was seized by the belt and dragged from Melynlas. A Huntsman tumbled with him to the ground. Closely grappled, Taran could not bring his sword into play. The Huntsman raised himself abruptly and thrust a knee against Taran's chest. The warrior's eyes glinted; he bared his teeth in a horrible grin as he raised a dagger.

The Huntsman's voice froze in the midst of a shout of triumph and he suddenly fell backward. Ellidyr, seeing Taran's plight, had brought down his sword in one powerful blow. Thrusting the life-less body aside, he heaved Taran to his feet.

For an instant their eyes met. Ellidyr's face, below a blood-stained mat of tawny hair, held a look of scorn and pride. He seemed about to speak, but turned quickly without a word and ran toward the fray.

In the grove there was a sudden moment of silence. Then a long sigh rippled among the attackers as though each man had drawn breath. Taran's heart sank as he remembered Gwydion's warning. With a roar, the Huntsmen renewed their attack with even greater ferocity, dashing themselves against the struggling companions in a surge of fury.

From astride Melynlas, Eilonwy fitted an arrow to her bow. Taran hurried to her side. "Do not slay them!" he cried. "Defend yourself but do not slay them!"

Just then a hairy, twiggy figure burst from the scrub. Gurgi had snatched up a sword nearly as tall as himself. His eyes shut tightly, he stamped his feet, shouted, and swung the weapon about him like a scythe. Furious as a hornet, he raced back and forth among the Huntsmen, bobbing up and down, his blade never still.

As the warriors sprang aside, Taran saw one of them clutch the air and spin head over heels. Another Huntsman doubled up and fell, pounded by invisible fists. He rolled across the ground in an attempt to escape the buffeting, but no sooner did he climb to his feet than a shouting, thrashing warrior was flung against him. The Huntsmen lashed out with their weapons, only to have them ripped from their hands and tossed into the scrub. Against this charge they fell back in alarm.

"Doli!" Taran cried. "It's Doli!"

Adaon took this moment to plunge forward. He seized Gurgi and hoisted him to Lluagor's back. "Follow me!" Adaon shouted. He turned his mount and shot past the struggling warriors.

Taran leaped to the back of Melynlas. With Eilonwy clinging to his belt, he bent low over the horse's silver mane. Arrows flew past him as Melynlas streaked ahead. Then the stallion was clear of the grove and pounding across open ground.

Ears back, Melynlas galloped past a line of trees. Dry leaves flew in a whirlwind beneath churning hooves, as the stallion sped to the brown crest of a hill. For a moment Taran dared to glance behind him. Below, a number of Huntsmen had separated from the band, and with great strides held to the track of the fleeing companions. They were swift, even as Gwydion had warned. In their jackets of bristling skins they seemed wild beasts rather than men, as they spread in a wide arc across the slope. As they ran, they called out to one another in a weird, wordless cry that echoed almost from the brooding crags of Dark Gate itself.

Cold with dread, Taran urged Melynlas on. Clumps of grass rose high among fallen tree trunks and withered branches. Ahead, Lluagor galloped down an embankment.

Adaon had brought them to a riverbed. Dark water lay in a few shallow pools, but for the most part it was dry and the clay banks rose high enough to offer concealment. Adaon reined in Lluagor and cast a quick glance behind him to make sure all had followed, then beckoned the companions to move forward. They set off at a rapid gait. The riverbed wound its way through high-standing firs and tattered alders, but after a little time the embankment fell away and a sparse forest became their only cover.

Although Melynlas did not slacken speed, Taran saw the pace had begun to tell on the other horses. Taran himself longed to rest. Doli's shaggy pony labored through the trees; the bard had ridden his own mount into a lather. Ellidyr's face was deathly pale, and he was bleeding heavily from his forehead.

They had not, as far as Taran could tell, stopped hastening westward, and Dark Gate lay some distance behind them, though its peaks no longer could be seen. Taran had hoped Adaon could have fallen back toward the path they had used earlier with Gwydion, but he knew now they were far from it and traveling still further.

Adaon led them to a dense thicket and signaled them to dismount. "We dare not stay here long," he warned. "There are few hiding places Arawn's hunters will not discover."

"Then stand and face them!" cried the bard. "A Fflam never shrinks!"

"Yes, yes! Gurgi will face them too!" put in Gurgi, although he seemed barely able to lift his head.

"We shall stand against them only if we must," Adaon said. "They are stronger now than before and will not tire as quickly as we will."

"We should make our stand now," Ellidyr cried. "Is this the

honor we gain from following Gwydion? To let ourselves be tracked down like animals? Or do you fear them too much?"

"I do not fear them," Taran retorted, "but it is no dishonor to shun them. This is what Gwydion himself would order."

Eilonwy, though exhausted and disheveled, had not lost the use of her tongue. "Oh be quiet, both of you!" she commanded. "You worry so much about honor when you'd be better off thinking of a way to get back to Caer Cadarn."

Taran, who had been crouched against a tree, raised his head from his hands. From a distance came a long, wavering cry. Another voice answered it, then another. "Are they giving up the hunt?" he asked. "Have we outrun them?"

Adaon shook his head. "I doubt it. They would not pursue us this far only to let us escape." He swung stiffly to Lluagor's back. "We must ride until we find a safer place to rest. We would have little hope if we let them come upon us now."

As Ellidyr strode to the weary Islimach, Taran took him by the arm. "You fought well, Son of Pen-Llarcau," he said quietly. "I think that I owe you my life."

Ellidyr turned to him with the same glance of contempt Taran had seen in the grove. "It is a small debt," he replied. "You value it more than I do."

They set out once again, moving deeper into the forest, as rapidly as their strength allowed. The day had turned heavy with dampness and chill. The sun was feeble, wrapped in ragged gray clouds. Their progress slowed in the tangle of underbrush and the wet leaves mired the struggling animals. Doli, who had been bent over his saddle, straightened abruptly. He looked sharply around him. Whatever he saw caused him to be strangely elated.

"There are Fair Folk here," he declared, as Taran rode up beside him.

"Are you sure?" Taran asked. "How do you know?"

Though he looked closely, he could see no difference between this stretch of forest and the one they had just passed through.

"How do I know? How do I know?" snapped Doli. "How do you know how to swallow your dinner?"

He kicked his heels against the pony's flanks and hurried past Adaon, who halted in surprise. Doli jumped down, and after examining several trees ran quickly to the ruins of an enormous hollow oak. He thrust his head inside and began shouting at the top of his voice.

Taran, too, dismounted. With Eilonwy at his heels, he ran to the tree, fearful the fatigue and strain of the day had at last driven the dwarf out of his wits.

"Ridiculous!" muttered Doli, pulling his head out of the tree. "I can't be that far wrong!"

He bent, sighted along the ground, and made incomprehensible calculations on his fingers. "It must be!" he cried. "King Eiddileg wouldn't let things run down this badly."

With that, he gave a number of furious kicks against the tree roots. Taran was sure the angry dwarf would have climbed into the tree itself had the opening in the trunk been larger.

"I'll report it," Doli cried, "yes, to Eiddileg himself! Unheard of! Impossible!"

"I don't know what you're doing," Eilonwy said, brushing past the dwarf and stepping up to the oak, "but if you'd tell us, we might be able to help you."

As the dwarf had done, she peered into the hollow trunk.

"I don't know who's down there," she called, "but we're up here and Doli wants to talk to you. At least you can answer! Do you hear me?"

Eilonwy turned away and shook her head. "They're impolite, whoever they are. That's worse than somebody shutting their eyes so you can't see them!"

A faint but distinct voice rose from the tree. "Go away," it said.

CHAPTER SIX

Gwystyl

Doli hurriedly pushed Eilonwy aside and ducked his head back into the tree trunk. He began shouting again, but the dead wood so muffled the sound that Taran could distinguish nothing of the conversation, which consisted mainly of long outbursts from the dwarf followed by brief and reluctant answers.

At length Doli straightened up and beckoned the others to follow. He set off at a great rate directly across the woodland, and after little more than a hundred paces, he jumped down a jutting bank. Taran, leading the dwarf's pony as well as Melynlas, hastened to join him. Adaon, Ellidyr, and the bard turned their mounts rapidly and were soon behind them.

The bank was so steeply inclined and overgrown that the horses could barely keep their footing. They stepped delicately among the brambles and exposed rocks. Islimach tossed her mane and whinnied nervously. The bard's mount came near to falling onto her haunches, and even Melynlas snorted a protest against the difficult slope.

By the time Taran reached a shelf of level ground, Doli had run to the protected face of the embankment and was fuming impatiently before a huge tangle of thornbushes. To Taran's amazement the brambles began to shudder as though being pushed from inside; then, with much scraping and snapping of twigs, the whole mass opened a crack.

"It's a way post of the Fair Folk," Eilonwy cried. "I knew they had them every which where, but leave it to good old Doli to find one!"

As Taran reached the dwarf's side, the portal opened wide enough for him to glimpse a figure behind it.

Doli peered inside. "So it's you, Gwystyl," he said. "I might have known."

"So it's you, Doli," a sad voice replied. "I wish you'd given me a little warning."

"Warning!" cried the dwarf. "I'll give you more than a warning if you don't open up! Eiddileg will hear of this. What good's a way post if you can't get into it when you have to? You know the rules: if any of the Fair Folk are in danger . . . Well, that's what we're in right now! On top of everything else, I could have shouted myself hoarse!" He gave a furious kick at the brambles.

The figure heaved a long and melancholy sigh, and the portal opened wider. Taran saw a creature which, at first glance, looked like a bundle of sticks with cobwebs floating at the top. He realized quickly the strange doorkeeper resembled certain of the Fair Folk he had once seen in Eiddileg's kingdom; only this individual seemed in a woeful state of disrepair.

Unlike Doli, Gwystyl was not of the dwarf kindred. Though taller, he was extremely thin. His sparse hair was long and stringy; his nose drooped wearily above his upper lip, which in turn drooped toward his chin in a most mournful expression. Wrinkles puckered his forehead; his eyes blinked anxiously; and he seemed on the verge of bursting into tears. Around his bent shoulders was draped a shabby, grimy robe, which he fingered nervously. He sniffed several times, sighed again, and grudgingly beckoned Doli to enter.

Gurgi and Fflewddur had come up behind Taran. Gwystyl, noticing them for the first time, gave a stifled moan.

"Oh, no," he said, "not humans. Another day, perhaps. I'm sorry, Doli, believe me. But not the humans."

"They're with me," snapped the dwarf. "They claim Fair Folk protection, and I'll see they get it."

Fflewddur's horse, slipping among the branches, whinnied loudly, and at this Gwystyl clapped a hand to his forehead.

"Horses!" he sobbed. "That's out of the question! Bring in your humans if you must. But not horses. Not horses today, Doli, I'm simply not up to horses today. Please, Doli," he moaned, "don't do this to me. I'm not well, not at all well, really. I couldn't think of it. All the snorting and stamping and big bony heads. Besides, there's no room. No room at all."

"What place is this?" Ellidyr questioned angrily. "Where have you led us, dwarf? My horse does not leave my side. Climb into this rathole, the rest of you. I shall guard Islimach myself."

"We can't leave the horses above ground," Doli told Gwystyl, who had already begun to retreat into the passageway. "Find room or make room," he ordered. "That's flat!"

Sniffing, groaning, shaking his head, Gwystyl with great reluctance heaved the doorway open to its full width.

"Very well," he sighed, "bring them in. Bring them all in. And if you know any others, invite them, too. It doesn't matter. I only suggested—an appeal to your generous heart, Doli. But I don't care now. It makes no difference."

Taran had begun to think Gwystyl had good reason for concern. The portal was barely high enough for the animals to pass through. Only with difficulty did Adaon's tall steed enter; and Islimach rolled her eyes frantically as the thorns tore at her flanks.

Once past this barrier, however, Taran saw they had entered a kind of gallery, long and low-ceilinged. One side of it was solid earth, the other a dense screen of thorns and branches impossible to see through but with enough cracks and crevices to admit a little air.

"You can put the horses in there, I suppose," sighed Gwystyl, fluttering his hands in the direction of the gallery. "I cleaned it not long ago. I wasn't expecting to have it turned into a stable. But go ahead, it doesn't make any difference."

Choking and sighing to himself, Gwystyl then led the companions through a damp-smelling passageway. On one side, Taran noticed, an alcove had been hollowed out; it was filled with roots, lichens, and mushrooms—the food stock, he guessed, of the melancholy inhabitant. Water dripped from the dirt roof or ran in rivulets down the wall. An odor of loam and dead leaves hung in the corridor. Farther on, the passage opened into a round chamber.

Here, a small fire of sod flickered on a tiny, ash-laden hearth, and gave out frequent puffs of sharp, nose-tingling smoke. A disorderly pallet of straw lay nearby. There was a broken table, two stools, and a vast number of bunches of herbs hung against the wall drying. Some attempt had been made to smooth the sides of the wall itself, but here and there the twisting fingers of roots poked through. Though the chamber was intensely hot and stuffy, Gwystyl shuddered and pulled his robe closer about his shoulders.

"Very cozy," Fflewddur remarked, coughing violently.

Gurgi hurried to the fireplace and, despite the smoke, flung himself down beside it. Adaon, who could barely stand to his full height, seemingly paid no attention to the disorder but went to Gwystyl and bowed courteously.

"We thank you for your hospitality," Adaon said. "We have been hard pressed."

"Hospitality!" snapped Doli. "We've seen precious little of that! Get along, Gwystyl, and fetch something to eat and drink."

"Oh, to be sure, to be sure," mumbled Gwystyl, "if you really want to take the time. When did you say you were leaving?"

Eilonwy gave a cry of delight. "Look, he has a tame crow!"

Near the fire, on a tree limb fashioned into a crude perch, crouched a heap of shadows which Taran realized was indeed a large crow. With Eilonwy, he hurried over to look at it. The crow resembled more a humpy ball with straggling tail feathers, feathers as wispy and disordered as Gwystyl's cobwebby hair. But its eyes were sharp and bright and they peered at Taran critically. With a few dry clicks, the bird polished its beak on the perch and cocked its head.

"It's a lovely crow," Eilonwy said, "though I've never seen one with feathers quite like it. They're unusual, but very handsome once you get used to them."

Since the crow did not object, Taran gently stirred the feathers around its neck and ran a finger under the bird's sharp and gleaming beak. With sudden sadness, he remembered the fledgling gwythaint he had befriended—long ago, it seemed—and wondered how the bird had fared. The crow, meantime, was enjoying an attention it evidently did not usually receive. It bobbed its head, blinked happily, and attempted to run its beak through Taran's hair.

"What's its name?" Eilonwy asked.

"Name?" answered Gwystyl. "Oh, his name is Kaw. Because of the noise he makes, you see. Something like that," he added vaguely.

"Kaw!" exclaimed Fflewddur, who had been watching with interest. "Excellent! How clever! I should never have thought of giving it a name like that." He nodded in pleasure and approval.

While Taran smoothed the feathers of the delighted crow, Adaon set about examining Ellidyr's wound. From a small wallet at his belt, he drew out a handful of dried herbs, which he ground into a powder.

"What," said Ellidyr, "are you a healer as well as a dreamer? If it does not trouble me, why should it trouble you?"

"If you do not choose to take it as a kindness," Adaon answered, unperturbed and continuing to treat the cut, "take it as a precaution. There is hard and dangerous travel before us. I would not have you fall ill and delay us."

"I shall not be the one to delay you," Ellidyr replied. "I would have stood my ground when the chance was offered. Now we have let ourselves be run to earth like foxes."

Gwystyl had been peering anxiously over Adaon's shoulder. "Do you have anything that might be useful for my condition?" he asked tremulously. "No, I don't suppose you do. Well, no matter. There's nothing to be done about the dampness and the drafts; no, they'll last longer than I, you can be sure," he added in a dismal voice.

"Stop muttering about the drafts," Doli ordered brusquely, "and think of some way to get us out of here safely. If you're in charge of a way post, you're supposed to be ready in emergencies." He turned away, furious. "I don't know what Eiddileg was thinking of when he put you here."

"I've often wondered that," Gwystyl agreed, with a melancholy sigh. "It's much too close to Annuvin for any decent kind of person to knock at your door—I don't mean any of you," he added hurriedly. "But it's bleak. Nothing of interest, really. No, Doli, I'm afraid there's nothing I can do for you. Except set you on your way as quickly as possible."

"What about the Huntsmen?" Taran put in. "If they're still tracking us . . ."

"Huntsmen?" Gwystyl turned a sickly greenish-white and his hands trembled. "How on earth did you come across them? I'm sorry to hear that. If I had known before, it might have been possible—oh, it's too late for that. They'll be all over the place now. No, really, you could have shown a little more consideration."

"You might think we wanted to have them after us!" cried Eilonwy, unable to curb her impatience. "That's like inviting a bee to come and sting you."

At the girl's outburst, Gwystyl shriveled up in his robe and looked more dismal than ever. He choked, wiped his forehead with a trembling hand, and let a large tear roll down his nose. "I didn't mean it that way, my dear child, believe me." Gwystyl sniffed. "I just don't see what's to be done about it—if anything at all. You've got yourself into a dreadful predicament. How or why, I'm sure I can't imagine."

"Gwydion had led us to attack Arawn," Taran began.

Gwystyl hurriedly raised a hand. "Don't tell me," he interrupted with an anxious frown. "Whatever it is, I don't want to hear about it. I'd rather not know. I don't want to be caught up in any of your mad schemes. Gwydion? I'm surprised *he*, at least, didn't know better. But it's to be expected, I suppose. There's no use complaining."

"Our quest is urgent," said Adaon, who had finished binding Ellidyr's wound and had come to stand near Gwystyl. "We ask you to do nothing to endanger yourself. I would not tell you the circumstances that brought us here, but without knowing them you cannot realize how desperately we need your help."

"We had come to seize the cauldron from Annuvin," Taran said.

"Cauldron?" murmured Gwystyl.

"Yes, the cauldron!" shouted the furious dwarf. "You pale grub! You lightless lightning bug! The cauldron of Arawn's Cauldron-Born!"

"Oh, *that* cauldron," Gwystyl answered feebly. "Forgive me, Doli, I was thinking of something else. When did you say you were going?"

The dwarf seemed on the verge of seizing Gwystyl by his robe and shaking him, but Adaon stepped forward and quickly explained what had occurred at Dark Gate.

"It's a shame," Gwystyl murmured, with a sorrowful sigh. "You should never have got mixed up with the thing. It's too late to think about that, I'm afraid. You'll just have to make the best of it. I don't envy you. Believe me, I don't. It's one of those unfortunate events."

"But you don't understand," Taran said. "We aren't mixed up with the cauldron. It isn't in Annuvin any more. Someone has already stolen it."

"Yes," said Gwystyl, with a gloomy look at Taran, "yes, I know."

CHAPTER SEVEN

Kaw

Taran stopped short. "You *know* that?" he asked in surprise. "Then why didn't you . . ."

Gwystyl gulped and darted nervous glances about him. "Oh, I know. But only in a very general way, you understand. I mean, I don't really know anything at all. Just the usual unfounded rumor you might expect to hear in a beastly place like this. Of no importance. Pay no attention to it."

"Gwystyl," said Doli sharply, "you know more about this than you let on. Now, out with it."

The gloomy creature flung his hands to his head and began moaning and rocking back and forth. "Do go away and let me alone," he sobbed. "I'm not well; I have so many tasks to finish, I shall never be caught up."

"You must tell us!" cried Taran. "Please," he added, lowering his voice, for the wretched Gwystyl had begun to shake violently, his eyes turning up as though he were about to have a fit. "Do not keep your knowledge from us. If you stay silent, our lives are risked for no purpose."

"Leave it alone," Gwystyl choked, fanning himself with an edge of his robe. "Don't bother with it. Forget it. That's the best thing you can do. Go back wherever you came from. Don't even think about it."

"How can we do that?" Taran cried. "Arawn won't rest until he has the cauldron again."

"Of course he won't rest," Gwystyl said. "He isn't resting now. That's exactly why you should drop the search and go quietly. You'll only stir up more trouble. And there's enough of that already."

"Then we'd better get back to Caer Cadarn and join Gwydion as quickly as we can," Eilonwy said.

"Yes, yes, by all means," broke in Gwystyl, with the first trace of eagerness Taran had glimpsed in this strange individual. "I only give you this advice for your own good. I'm glad, very glad, you've seen fit to follow it. Now, of course," he added, almost brightly, "you'll want to be on your way. Very wise of you. I, unhappily, have to stay here. I envy you, I really do. But—that's the way of it, and there's little anyone can do. A pleasure meeting you all. Good-bye."

"Good-bye?" cried Eilonwy. "If we put our noses above ground and the Huntsmen are waiting for us—yes, it will be good-bye indeed! Doli says it's your duty to help us. And with that, you haven't done a thing. Except sigh and moan! If this is the best the Fair Folk can manage, why, I'd rather be up a tree with my toes tied together!"

Gwystyl clutched his head again. "Please, please, don't shout. I'm not up to shouting today. Not after the horses. One of you can go and see if the Huntsmen are still there. Not that it will really do any good, for they might have just stepped away for a moment."

"I wonder who'll do that?" muttered the dwarf. "Good old Doli, of course. I thought I'd done with making myself invisible."

"I could give all of you a little something," Gwystyl went on, "not that it will do much good. It's a kind of powder I've put by in case of need. I was saving it for emergencies."

"What do you call this, you clot!" Doli growled.

"Yes, well, I meant, ah, more for personal emergencies," Gwystyl explained, paling. "But it doesn't matter about me. You can have it. Take all of it, go ahead.

"You put it on your feet, or whatever you walk on—I mean hooves and so forth," Gwystyl added. "It doesn't work too well, hardly much sense in bothering. Because it wears off. Naturally, if you're walking on it, it *would* do that. However, it will hide your tracks for a while."

"That's what we need," said Taran. "Once we throw the Huntsmen off our trail, I think we can outrun them."

"I'll get some," Gwystyl said with eagerness. "It won't take a moment."

As he made to leave the chamber, however, Doli took him by the arm. "Gwystyl," said the dwarf severely, "you have a skulking, sneaking look in your eyes. You might hoodwink my friends. But don't forget you're also dealing with one of the Fair Folk. I have a feeling," Doli added, tightening his grip, "you're far too anxious to see us gone. I'm beginning to wonder, if I squeezed you a little, what more might come out."

At this, Gwystyl rolled up his eyes and fainted away. The dwarf had to haul him upright, while Taran and the others fanned him.

At length Gwystyl opened one eye. "Sorry," he gasped. "Not myself today. Too bad about the cauldron. One of those unfortunate things."

The crow, who had been watching all this activity, turned a beady glance on his owner and flapped his wings with such vigor that Gurgi roused himself in alarm.

"Orddu!" Kaw croaked.

Fflewddur turned in surprise. "Well, can you imagine that! He didn't say 'kaw' at all. At least it didn't seem that way to me. I could have sworn he said something like 'or-do.' "

"Orwen!" croaked Kaw. "Orgoch!"

"There," said Fflewddur, looking at the bird with fascination. "He did it again."

"It's strange," agreed Taran. "It sounded like orduorwenorgoch! And look at him, running back and forth on his perch. Do you think we've upset him?"

"He acts as if he wants to tell us something," began Eilonwy.

Gwystyl's face, meanwhile, had turned the color of ancient cheese.

"*You* may not want us to know," said Doli, roughly seizing the terrified Gwystyl, "but *he* does. This time, Gwystyl, I really mean to squeeze you."

"No, no, Doli, please don't do that," wailed Gwystyl. "Don't give him another thought. He does odd things; I've tried to teach him better habits, but it doesn't do any good."

A flood of Gwystyl's pleading and moaning followed, but the dwarf paid it no heed, and began to carry out his threat.

"No," squealed Gwystyl. "No squeezing. Not today. Listen to me, Doli," he added, his eyes crossing and uncrossing frantically, "if I tell you, will you promise to go away?"

Doli nodded and relaxed his grip.

"All Kaw meant to say," Gwystyl went on hurriedly, "is that the cauldron is in the hands of Orddu, Orwen, and Orgoch. That's all.

It's a shame, but there's *certainly* nothing to be done about it. It hardly seemed worth mentioning."

"Who are Orddu, Orwen, and Orgoch?" Taran asked. His excitement and impatience were getting the better of him, too, and he was sorely tempted to aid Doli in squeezing Gwystyl.

"*Who* are *they?*" murmured Gwystyl. "You had better ask *what* are they?"

"Very well," cried Taran, "what are they?"

"I don't know," replied Gwystyl. "It's hard to say. It doesn't matter; they've got the cauldron and you might as well let it rest there." He shuddered violently. "Don't meddle with them; there's no earthly use in it."

"Whoever they are, or whatever they are," cried Taran, turning to the rest of the company, "I say find them and take the cauldron. That's what we set out to do, and we should not turn back now. Where do they live?" he asked Gwystyl.

"Live?" asked Gwystyl with a frown. "They don't live. Not exactly. It's all very vague. I really don't know."

Kaw flapped his wings again. "Morva!" he croaked.

"I mean," Gwystyl moaned, as the angry Doli reached for him again, "they stay in the Marshes of Morva. Exactly where, I have no idea, no idea at all. That's the trouble. You'll never find them. And if you do, which you won't, you'll wish you never had." Gwystyl wrung his bony hands, and his trembling features indeed held a look of deepest dread.

"I have heard of the Marshes of Morva," Adaon said. "They lie to the west of here. How far, I do not know."

"I do!" interrupted Fflewddur. "A good day's journey, I should say. I once came upon them during my wanderings. I recall them quite clearly. Unpleasant stretch of country and quite terrifying. Not that it bothered me, of course. Undaunted, I strode through . . ."

A harp string snapped abruptly with a resounding twang.

"I went around them," the bard corrected himself hurriedly. "Dreadful, smelly, ugly-looking fens they were. But," he added, "if that's where the cauldron is, then I say with Taran: go there! A Fflam never hesitates!"

"A Fflam never hesitates to open his mouth," put in Doli. "Gwystyl is telling the truth for once, I'm sure of it. I've heard tales, back in Eiddileg's realm, of those—whatever you call thems. And they weren't pleasant. Nobody knows much about them. Or, if they do, they aren't telling."

"You should pay attention to Doli," interrupted Eilonwy, turning impatiently to Taran. "I don't see how you can even think about getting the cauldron away from whoever has it—and not even knowing *whatever* has it.

"Besides," Eilonwy went on, "Gwydion ordered us to meet him at Caer Cadarn, and if my memory hasn't got holes in it from all the nonsense I've been hearing, he didn't say a word about going off in the opposite direction."

"You don't understand," Taran retorted. "When he told us to meet him, he was going to plan a new search. He didn't know we would find the cauldron."

"In the first place," Eilonwy said, "you haven't found the cauldron."

"But we know where it is!" cried Fflewddur. "That's just as good!"

"And in the second place," Eilonwy continued, ignoring the bard, "if you've got any news about it, the only wise thing is to find Gwydion and tell him what you know."

"That's sense," put in Doli. "We'll have enough trouble getting to Caer Cadarn without splashing around in swamps on a wild goose chase. You listen to her. She's the only one, outside of myself, who has any notion of what ought to be done."

Taran hesitated. "It may be," he said, after a pause, "that we would be wiser returning to Gwydion. King Morgant and his warriors can lend us their strength."

He spoke these words with some effort; in the back of his mind he yearned to find the cauldron, to bring it in triumph to Gwydion. Nevertheless, he could not deny to himself that Eilonwy and Doli had proposed the surer plan.

"It seems to me, then," he began. But he had no sooner started to agree with Doli than Ellidyr thrust his way to the fireside.

"Pig-boy," Ellidyr said, "you have chosen well. Return with your friends and let us make our parting here."

"Parting?" asked Taran, puzzled.

"Do you think I would turn my back now, when the prize is nearly won?" Ellidyr said coldly. "Go your way, pig-boy, and I shall go mine—to the Marshes of Morva themselves. Wait for me at Caer Cadarn," Ellidyr added with a scornful smile. "Warm your courage beside the fire. I shall bring the cauldron there."

Taran's eyes flashed with anger at Ellidyr's words. The thought that Ellidyr should find the cauldron was more than he could bear.

"I shall warm my courage, Son of Pen-Llarcau," he cried, "in whatever fire you choose! Go back, the rest of you, if that's what you want. I was a fool to listen to the thoughts of a girl!"

Eilonwy gave a furious shriek. Doli raised a hand in protest, but Taran cut him short. He was calmer now that his first anger had passed. "This is not a game of courage," he said. "I would be twice a fool, and so should we all, to be goaded by an idle taunt.

This much, at least, I have learned from Gwydion. But there is also this: Arawn seeks the cauldron even now. We do not dare lose the time it would take to bring help. If he finds the cauldron before we do . . ."

"And if he doesn't?" put in Doli. "How do you know he knows where it is? And if he doesn't know, how long will it take him to find out? A merry while, I'll be bound, even with all his Cauldron-Born and Huntsmen and gwythaints, and what have you! There's a risk either way, any clodpole can see that. But if you ask me, there's more risk than otherwise if you go popping off into the Marshes of Morva."

"And you, Taran of Caer Dallben," said Eilonwy, "you're only making excuses for some harebrained idea of your own. You've been talking and talking and you've forgotten one thing. You're not the one to decide anything; and neither are you, Ellidyr. Adaon commands you both, *if* I'm not mistaken."

Taran flushed at Eilonwy's reminder. "Forgive me, Adaon," he said, bowing his head. "I did not intend to disobey your orders. The choice is yours."

Adaon, who had been listening silently near the fire, shook his head. "No," he said quietly, "this choice cannot be mine. I have said nothing for or against your plan; the decision is greater than I dare make."

"But why?" cried Taran. "I don't understand," he said quickly and with concern. "Of all of us, you know best what to do."

Adaon turned his gray eyes toward the fire. "Perhaps you will understand one day. For now, choose your path, Taran of Caer Dallben," he said. "Wherever it may lead, I promise you my help."

Taran drew back and stood silent a moment, filled with distress and uneasiness. It was not fear touching his heart, but the wordless sorrow of dry leaves rushing desolate before the wind. Adaon continued to watch the dance of the flames.

"I shall go to the Marshes of Morva," Taran said.

Adaon nodded. "So it shall be."

No one spoke then. Even Ellidyr made no reply; he bit his lips and fingered the hilt of his sword.

"Well," said Doli at last, "I suppose I might as well go along, too. Do what I can. But it's a mistake, I warn you."

"Mistake?" cried the jubilant bard. "By no means! I wouldn't be kept away from it!"

"And I certainly won't," declared Eilonwy. "Someone has to make sure there are at least a few of us with good sense along. Marshes! Ugh! If you insist on making fools of yourselves, I wish you'd picked a drier way."

"And Gurgi will help!" shouted Gurgi, springing to his feet. "Yes, yes, with seekings and peekings!"

"Gwystyl," said Doli, with a look of resignation, "you might as well go and fetch that powder you were talking about."

While Gwystyl eagerly rummaged through the alcove, the dwarf drew a deep breath and flickered out of sight. He was back after some length of time, fully visible and looking furious, his ears trembling and rimmed with blue.

"There's five Huntsmen camped over the rise," he said. "They've settled down for the—oh, my ears—night. If that powder is any good, we can be well away before they even know we've been here."

The companions dusted their feet and the hooves of their steeds with a black substance Gwystyl distributed from a moldering sack.

He seemed almost gleeful, as Taran untethered Melynlas and led the horse from behind the screen of brambles.

"Good-bye, good-bye," muttered Gwystyl. "I hate to see you waste your time, not to mention your lives. But that's the way of it, I suppose. Here today, gone tomorrow, and what's anyone to do about it? Good-bye. I hope we meet again. But not soon. Good-bye."

With that, the portal shut. Taran took a firmer grip on the bridle of Melynlas and the companions moved silently into the forest.

CHAPTER EIGHT

A Stone in the Shoe

Outside the way post, night had already fallen; the sky was clear once more, but the chill had deepened. Adaon and Fflewddur held a hurried council on which path to follow, and agreed the company should ride westward until dawn, conceal themselves and sleep, then turn due south. As before, Eilonwy shared Melynlas with Taran, and Gurgi clung to the back of Lluagor.

Fflewddur had offered to lead the way, claiming he had never been lost and could find the Marshes with his eyes shut; after two harp strings had snapped, he reconsidered and gave up his position to Adaon. Doli, still muttering angrily about his buzzing ears, rode last, as rear guard, although he flatly refused to make himself invisible no matter what the circumstances.

Ellidyr had spoken to no one since leaving the melancholy Gwystyl, and Taran had seen the cold rage in his eyes after the companions' decision to press on to the Marshes of Morva.

"I think he really would have tried to bring back the cauldron by himself," Taran said to Eilonwy. "And you know how much chance he would have had alone. That's the kind of childish thing I'd have done when I was an Assistant Pig-Keeper."

"You're still an Assistant Pig-Keeper," answered Eilonwy. "You're going to these silly swamps because of Ellidyr, and anything else you say is pure nonsense. Don't tell me it wouldn't have been wiser to find Gwydion. But no, you have to decide the other way and drag the rest of us along."

Taran did not reply. Eilonwy's words stung him—all the more because he had begun to regret his own decision. Now the companions had set off, doubts tormented him and his heart was heavy. Taran could not forget the strange tone in Adaon's voice and sought again and again to understand why he had turned from a choice rightfully his. He jogged Melynlas closer to Adaon and leaned from the saddle.

"I am troubled," he said in a low voice, "and I wonder now if we should not turn back. I fear you have kept something from me, and had I known what it was, I would have chosen otherwise."

If Adaon shared Taran's doubts, he showed no sign. In the saddle, he rode unbowed, as though he had gained new strength and the weariness of the journey could no longer touch him. On his face was a look Taran had never seen before and could not fathom. In it was pride, yet more than that; for it held, as well, a light that seemed almost joyous.

After a long pause Adaon said, "There is a destiny laid on us to do what we must do, though it is not always given to us to see it."

"I think you see many things," Taran replied quietly, "many things which you tell no one. It has long been in my mind," he went on, with much hesitation, "and now more than ever—the dream you had, the last night in Caer Dallben. You saw Ellidyr and King Morgant; to me, you foretold I would grieve. But what did you dream of yourself?"

Adaon smiled. "Is that what troubles you? Very well, I shall tell you. I saw myself in a glade; and though winter lay all around, it was warm and sunlit. Birds called and flowers sprang up from bare stones."

"Your dream was beautiful," said Eilonwy, "but I can't guess its meaning."

Taran nodded. "Yes, it is beautiful. I feared it had been unhappy and for that reason you chose not to speak of it."

Adaon said nothing more and Taran fell back into his own thoughts, still finding no reassurance. Melynlas moved ahead, sure-footed despite the darkness. The stallion was able to avoid the loose stones and fallen branches that lay across the winding path, even without Taran's hands on the reins. His eyes heavy with fatigue, Taran leaned forward and patted the stallion's power-ful neck.

"Follow the way, my friend," Taran murmured. "Surely you know it better than I do."

At daybreak Adaon raised his hand and signaled a halt. Throughout the night they had ridden, as it seemed to Taran, down a long series of descending slopes. They were still in the Forest of Idris, but here the ground had leveled a little. Many of the trees were yet covered with leaves; the undergrowth was thicker; the land less stark than the hills around Dark Gate. Doli, his pony snorting white mist, galloped up to report no sign of the Huntsmen on their trail.

"How long that sallow mealworm's powder lasts I couldn't guess," said the dwarf. "And I don't think it'll do us that much good anyway. If Arawn's looking for the cauldron, he's going to look hard and close. The Huntsmen must know we've come in this general direction. If enough of them keep after us, sooner or later they're bound to find us. That Gwystyl—for all the help he's been! Humph! And his crow, too. Humph! I wish we hadn't run into either of them."

Ellidyr had dismounted and was anxiously studying Islimach's left foreleg. Taran, too, swung down and went to Ellidyr's side. The horse whinnied and rolled her eyes as he approached.

"She has gone lame," Taran said. "Unless we can help her, I fear she will not be able to hold the pace."

"I need no pig-boy to tell me that," answered Ellidyr. He bent and examined the mare's hoof with a gentleness of touch which surprised Taran.

"If you lightened her burden," Taran suggested, "it might ease her for a while. Fflewddur can take you up behind him."

Ellidyr straightened, his eyes black and bitter. "Do not give me counsel on my own steed. Islimach can go on. And so she will."

Nevertheless, as Ellidyr turned away, Taran saw his face fill with lines of worry. "Let me look at her," Taran said. "Perhaps I can find the trouble." He knelt and reached toward Islimach's foreleg.

"Do not touch her," cried Ellidyr. "She will not abide a stranger's hands."

Islimach reared and bared her teeth. Ellidyr laughed scornfully. "Learn for yourself, pig-boy," he said. "Her hooves are sharp as knives, as you shall see."

Taran rose and grasped Islimach's bridle. For a moment, as the horse lunged, he feared she would indeed trample him. Islimach's eyes were round with terror; she whickered and struck out at him. A hoof glanced against his shoulder, but Taran did not loosen his hold. He reached up and put a hand to Islimach's long, bony head.

The mare shuddered, but Taran spoke quietly and soothingly to her. She tossed her mane, the straining muscles relaxed; the reins went loose and she made no attempt to draw away.

Without stopping the flow of reassuring words, Taran raised her hoof. As he had suspected, there was a small, jagged stone wedged far back behind the shoe. He drew his knife. Islimach trembled, but Taran worked quickly and deftly. The stone came free and fell to the ground.

"This has happened even to Melynlas," Taran explained, patting the roan's flank. "There's a place deep in the hoof—anyone can miss it if they don't know. It was Coll who showed me how to find it."

Ellidyr's face was livid. "You have tried to steal honor from me, pig-boy," he said through clenched teeth. "Will you now rob me of my horse?"

Taran had expected no thanks, but the angry thrust of Ellidyr's words took him aback. Ellidyr's hand was on his sword. Taran felt a surge of answering anger, a flush rising to his cheeks, but he turned away.

"Your honor is your own," Taran answered coldly, "and so is your steed. What stone is in your shoe, Prince of Pen-Llarcau?"

He strode to his companions, who had taken cover in the tangle of brush. Gurgi had already opened the wallet and was proudly distributing its contents. "Yes, yes!" Gurgi cried gleefully, "crunchings and munchings for all! Thanks to generous, kindhearted Gurgi! He will not let brave warriors suffer bellies filled only with howlings and growlings!"

Ellidyr remained behind, patting Islimach's neck and murmuring in the roan's ear. Since he made no move to join the companions at their meal, Taran called out to him. But the Prince of Pen-Llarcau only gave him a bitter glance and remained with Islimach.

"That foul-tempered nag is the only thing he cares about," muttered the bard, "and as far as I can see, the only thing that cares about him. They're two of a kind, if you ask me."

Adaon, sitting a little apart from the others, called Taran to him. "I commend your patience," he said. "The black beast spurs Ellidyr cruelly."

"I think he'll feel better once we find the cauldron," Taran said. "There will be glory enough for all to share."

Adaon smiled gravely. "Is there not glory enough in living the days given to us? You should know there is adventure in simply being among those we love and the things we love, and beauty, too.

"But I would speak to you of another matter," Adaon went on. His handsome face, usually tranquil, was clouded. "I have few possessions, for I count them of little importance. But these few I treasure: Lluagor, my packets of healing herbs, and this," he said, touching the clasp at his throat, "the brooch I wear, a precious gift from Arianllyn, my betrothed. Should any ill befall me, they are yours. I have watched you closely, Taran of Caer Dallben. In all my journeys I have met no one else to whom I would rather entrust them."

"Do not speak of ill befalling you," Taran cried. "We are companions and protect one another against dangers. Besides, Adaon, your friendship is gift enough for me."

"Nevertheless," Adaon replied, "we cannot know all the future holds. Will you accept them?"

Taran nodded.

"It is well," Adaon said. "Now my heart is lighter."

After the meal it was decided they would rest until midday. Ellidyr made no comment when Adaon ordered him to stand the first watch. Taran rolled up in his cloak under the protection of a bush. Exhausted by the journey, and by his own doubts and fears, he slept heavily.

The sun was high when he opened his eyes. He sat up with a start, realizing his turn at guard had almost passed. Around him, the companions still slept.

"Ellidyr," he called, "why didn't you wake me?" He rose hurriedly to his feet. There was no sign of Ellidyr or Islimach.

Taran hastily roused the others. He ran a little distance into the trees, then circled back. "He's gone!" Taran cried. "He's gone after the cauldron alone. He said he would and now he's done it!"

"Stolen a march on us, has he?" grumbled Doli. "Well, we'll catch up to him, and if we don't—that's his concern. He doesn't know where he's going and, for the matter of that, neither do we."

"Good riddance to him," said Fflewddur. "If we have any kind of luck at all, we may not see him again."

For the first time Taran saw deep alarm in Adaon's face. "We must overtake him quickly," Adaon said. "Ellidyr's pride and ambition swallow him up. I fear to think what might happen should the cauldron come into his hands."

They set off with all possible haste. Adaon soon found Ellidyr's trail leading southward. "I was hoping he might have got disgusted with the whole business and gone home," said Fflewddur, "but there's no doubt of it, he's heading for Morva."

Despite their speed, the companions saw no sign of Ellidyr himself. They pressed on, urging the last strength from the laboring horses, until they were obliged to halt for breath. A cold wind had risen, swirling the leaves in great circles above their heads.

"I do not know if we can overtake him," Adaon said. "He rides as swiftly as we, and he is nearly a quarter day's journey ahead of us."

His heart pounding, Taran flung himself from Melynlas and slumped to the ground. He cradled his head in his hands. From a distance came the shrill call of a bird, the first birdsong he had heard since leaving Caer Dallben.

"That is not the true speech of a bird," Adaon cried, springing to his feet. "The Huntsmen have found us."

Without awaiting Adaon's order, the dwarf raced in the direction of the Huntsmen's signal. As Taran watched, Doli vanished before his eyes. Adaon drew his sword. "This time we must stand against them," he said. "We can run from them no longer." Quickly he commanded Taran, Eilonwy, and Gurgi to ready their bows, while he and the bard mounted their horses.

Within moments the dwarf was back again. "Five Huntsmen!" he cried. "Go on, the rest of you. I'll play them the same trick."

"No," said Adaon. "I do not trust it to work again. Hurry, follow me."

He led them through a clearing and halted at the far side. "Here we make our stand," Adaon said to Taran. "As soon as they come in sight, Fflewddur, Doli, and I will charge them from the flank. When they turn to give battle, loose your arrows."

Adaon swung around to face the clearing. In another instant the Huntsmen burst from cover. They had no sooner taken a stride forward than Adaon, with a great cry, urged his horse across the ground. Doli and the bard galloped beside him. Even as Taran drew his bow, Adaon was in the midst of the Huntsmen, striking left and right with his blade. The dwarf had pulled the stubby axe from his belt and chopped furiously at his enemies. Surprised by the fierce attack, the Huntsmen spun about to engage the riders.

Taran loosed his arrow, and heard the shafts of Eilonwy and Gurgi whistle past him. The flight of all three went wild, snatched by the wind and skittering among the dry bushes. Shouting madly, Gurgi fitted another arrow to his bow. Three Huntsmen pressed toward Fflewddur and the dwarf, forcing them into a thicket. Adaon's sword flashed and rang against the weapons of his assailants.

Now Taran dared not loose another shaft for fear of hitting one of the companions. "We are fighting uselessly," he cried, and flung his bow to the ground. He unsheathed his sword and ran to Adaon's aid.

One of the Huntsmen shifted his attack to Taran, who struck out at him with all his strength. His blow glanced from the jacket of animal skins, but the Huntsman lost his footing and dropped to earth. Taran stepped forward. He had forgotten the vicious daggers of the Huntsmen until he saw the man raise himself and snatch at his belt.

Taran froze with horror. In front of him, he saw the snarling face with its crimson brand, the arm uplifted to throw the blade. Suddenly Lluagor was between him and the Huntsman. Adaon rose in the saddle and swept down with his sword. As the Huntsman toppled, the knife flew glittering through the air.

Adaon gasped and dropped his weapon. He slumped over Lluagor's mane, clutching the dagger in his breast.

With a cry of anguish, Taran caught him as he was about to fall.

"Fflewddur! Doli!" Taran shouted. "To us! Adaon is wounded!"

CHAPTER NINE

The Brooch

Fflewddur's horse reared as the Huntsmen turned their attack against him. The death of one of their band had roused the enemy to even greater violence and frenzy.

"Take him to safety!" cried the bard. With a mighty leap his steed cleared the bushes and streaked into the forest. The dwarf on his pony followed. With a shout of rage, the remaining Huntsmen pursued them.

Taran seized Lluagor's bridle and, while Adaon clung to the horse's mane, raced toward the edge of the clearing. Eilonwy ran to meet them. Between them, they kept Adaon from falling and tore their way into the undergrowth. Gurgi, leading Melynlas, hurried after them.

They ran blindly, stumbling through brambles and harsh nets of dead vines. The wind had risen, cold and biting as a winter gale, but the forest opened a little, and as the ground dipped, they found themselves in a protected hollow in a glade of alders.

From the back of Lluagor, Adaon raised his head and gestured for them to stop. His face was gray and drawn, his black hair damp on his brow. "Put me down," he murmured. "Leave me. I can go no farther. How do the bard and Doli fare?"

"They have led the Huntsmen away from us," Taran answered quickly. "We are safe here for a while. I know Doli can throw them off our trail, and Fflewddur will help him. They'll join us again somehow, I'm sure. Rest now. I'll fetch your medicines from the saddlebags."

Carefully, they lifted Adaon from his steed and carried him to a hillock. While Eilonwy brought the leather water flask, Taran and Gurgi unharnessed Lluagor and set the saddle under Adaon's head. The wind howled above the trees, but this sheltered spot, by contrast, seemed warm. The driven clouds broke away; the sun turned the branches to gold.

Adaon raised himself. His gray eyes scanned the glade and he nodded briefly. "Yes, this is a fair place. I shall rest here."

"We shall heal your wound," Taran replied, hastily opening a packet of herbs. "You'll soon be comfortable, and if we must move, we can make a litter from branches and sling it between our horses."

"I am comfortable enough," Adaon said. "The pain has gone and it is pleasant here, as warm as spring."

At Adaon's words, Taran's heart filled with terror. The quiet glade, the sun on the alders, seemed suddenly menacing. "Adaon!" he cried in alarm. "This is what you dreamed!"

"It is much like it," Adaon answered quietly.

"You knew, then!" cried Taran. "You knew there would be peril for you. Why did you not speak of it before? I would never have sought the Marshes. We could have turned back."

Adaon smiled. "It is true. Indeed, that is why I dared not speak. I have yearned to be again at the side of my beloved Arianllyn, and my thoughts are with her now. But had I chosen to return, I would ever wonder whether my choice was made through wisdom or following the wishes of my own heart. I see this is as it must be, and the destiny laid upon me. I am content to die here."

"You saved my life," Taran cried. "You will not lose your own life for me. We shall find our way to Caer Cadarn and Gwydion."

Adaon shook his head. He put his hand to his throat and undid the iron clasp at the collar of his jacket. "Take this," he said. "Guard it well. It is a small thing, but more valuable than you know."

"I must refuse," answered Taran with a smile that ill concealed his anxiety. "Such would be the gift of a dying man. But you shall live, Adaon."

"Take it," Adaon repeated. "This is not my command to you, but the wish of one friend to another." He pressed the brooch into Taran's unwilling hand.

Eilonwy had come with water to steep the herbs. Taran took it from her and knelt again beside Adaon.

Adaon's eyes had closed. His face was calm; his hand lay outstretched and open on the ground.

And thus he died.

When their grief abated a little, the companions hollowed out a grave, lining it with flat stones. Wrapping him in his cloak, they lowered Adaon into the earth and laid the turf gently over him, while Lluagor whinnied plaintively and pawed the dry ground. Then they raised a mound of boulders. In a sheltered corner of the glade, Eilonwy found handfuls of small flowers still untouched by the frost. These she scattered on the grave, where they fell among the crevices and seemed to spring from the rocks themselves.

They remained there silently until nightfall, without a sign of Fflewddur or Doli. "We shall wait for them until dawn," Taran said. "Beyond that, we dare not stay. I fear we have lost more than one gallant friend."

"Adaon warned that I would grieve," he murmured to himself. "And so I do, thrice over."

Too burdened with sorrow, too weary even to set a guard, they huddled in their cloaks and slept. Like his spirit, Taran's dreams were confused, filled with dismay and fear. In them, he saw the mournful faces of the companions, the calm face of Adaon. He saw Ellidyr seized by a black beast that sank its claws into him and gripped him until Ellidyr cried out in torment.

The restless images gave way to a vast sweep of meadow, where Taran ran through grasses shoulder high, desperately seeking a path he could not find. Overhead, a gray bird fluttered and spread its wings. He followed it and a path opened at his feet.

He saw, too, a turbulent stream with a great boulder in the midst of it. On the boulder lay Fflewddur's harp, which played of itself as the wind stirred the strings.

Taran was running, then, through a trackless marsh. A bear and two wolves set upon him and made to rend him with their fangs. Terrified, he sprang into a dark pool, but the water suddenly turned to dry land. The enraged beasts snarled and leaped after him.

He woke with a start, his heart pounding. The night had barely ended; the first streaks of dawn rose above the glade. Eilonwy stirred; Gurgi whimpered in his sleep. Taran bowed his head and put his face in his hands. The dream lay heavily upon him; he could still see the gaping jaws of a wolf and the sharp, white teeth. He shuddered. He knew he must decide now whether to return to Caer Cadarn or seek the Marshes of Morva.

Taran looked beside him at the sleeping figures of Gurgi and Eilonwy. In little more than a day, the companions had been scattered like leaves, and there remained only this pitifully small band, itself lost and driven. How could they hope to find the cauldron? Taran doubted they would even be able to save their own lives; yet the journey to Caer Cadarn would be as perilous as this quest, perhaps more so. Nevertheless, a choice had to be made.

He rose after a time and saddled the horses. Eilonwy was now awake and Gurgi was poking a tousled, twig-covered head from the folds of his cloak.

"Hurry," Taran ordered. "We'd better get an early start before the Huntsmen overtake us."

"They'll find us soon enough," Eilonwy said. "They're probably as thick as burdock between here and Caer Cadarn."

"We are going to the Marshes," Taran said, "not Caer Cadarn."

"What?" Eilonwy cried. "Are you still thinking about those wretched swamps? Do you seriously think we can find that cauldron, let alone haul it back from wherever it is?

"On the other hand," Eilonwy went on, before Taran could answer her, "I suppose it's the only thing we can do, now that you've got us in the stew. And there's no telling what Ellidyr has in mind. If you hadn't made him jealous over a silly horse . . ."

"I feel pity for Ellidyr," Taran answered. "Adaon once told me he saw a black beast on Ellidyr's shoulders. Now I understand a little what he meant."

"Well," remarked Eilonwy, "I'm surprised to hear you say that. But it was kindhearted of you to help Islimach; I'm really glad you did. I'm sure you meant well, and that's encouraging in itself. It does make a person think there might be some hope for you after all."

Taran did not reply, for he was still anxious and oppressed, although the disturbing dreams had already begun to fade. He swung astride Melynlas; Gurgi and Eilonwy shared Lluagor; and the companions swiftly rode from the glade.

It was Taran's intention to head southward, hoping somehow to come upon the Marshes of Morva within another day; although he admitted to himself that he had no more than a vague idea of their distance or exact location.

The day was bright and crisp. As Melynlas cantered over the frosty ground, Taran caught sight of a glittering, dew-covered web on a hawthorn branch and of the spider busily repairing it. Taran was aware, strangely, of vast activities along the forest trail. Squirrels prepared their winter hoard; ants labored in their earthen castles. He could see them clearly, not so much with his eyes but in a way he had never known before.

The air itself bore special scents. There was a ripple, sharp and clear, like cold wine. Taran knew, without stopping to think, that a north wind had just begun to rise. Yet in the middle of this he noticed another scent mingled through. He turned Melynlas toward it.

"Since you're leading us," Eilonwy remarked, "I wonder if it would be too much to expect you to know where you're going."

"There is water nearby," Taran said. "We shall need to fill our flasks . . ." He hesitated, puzzled. "Yes, there is a stream," he murmured, "I'm sure of it. We must go there."

Nevertheless, he could not quite overcome his surprise when, after a short while, they indeed came upon a swift running brook winding its way through a stand of rowans. They rode to its bank. With a cry, Taran sharply reined in Melynlas. On a rock in the middle of the stream sat Fflewddur, cooling his bare feet in the water.

The bard leaped up and splashed across to greet the companions. Though haggard and worn, he appeared unwounded. "Now there's a stroke of luck, my finding you—your finding me, rather. I hate to admit it, but I'm lost. Completely. Got turned around somehow after Doli and I began leading the Huntsmen a chase. Tried to make my way back to you and got lost even more. How is Adaon? I'm glad you managed to . . ." The bard stopped. Taran's expression told him what had happened. Fflewddur shook his head sadly. "There are few like Adaon," he said. "We can ill afford the loss. Nor the loss of our good old Doli.

"I'm not sure what happened," Fflewddur went on. "All I know is that we were galloping at top speed. You should have seen him! He rode like a madman, popping invisible and back again, the Huntsmen racing after him. If it hadn't been for him, they'd have dragged me down for certain. They're stronger than ever, now. Then my horse fell. That is to say," the bard hastily added, as his harp strings tensed and jangled, "*I* fell off. Fortunately, by that time Doli had led them well away. At the rate he was going . . ." Fflewddur sighed heavily. "What has befallen him since then, I do not know."

The bard bound up his leggings. He had walked all the distance and was quite pleased to be riding once again. Gurgi mounted behind him on Lluagor. Taran and Eilonwy rode Melynlas. The bard's news lowered Taran's spirits further, for he realized now there was little chance of Doli rejoining them. Nevertheless, he continued to lead the companions southward.

Until he should recognize a landmark, Fflewddur agreed this was the only course. "The trouble is," he explained, "if we veer too far south, we'll simply end up in the sea and miss the Marshes altogether."

Taran himself could offer no suggestions. Downcast, he gave Melynlas rein and made little effort to guide the stallion. The trees thinned out behind him and the companions entered a wide, rolling meadow. Taran, half-dozing in the saddle, his cloak wrapped around his shoulders, roused himself uneasily. The meadow, with its high grass stretching all around them, was familiar. He had seen it before; where, he could not quite remember. He fingered Adaon's clasp at his throat. Suddenly, with fear and excitement, he understood. His hands trembled at the discovery. Taran glanced overhead. A gray bird circled, glided downward on outspread wings, then flew rapidly across the fields and disappeared from sight.

"That was a marsh bird," Taran said, quickly turning Melynlas. "If we follow this way," he added, pointing in the direction of the bird's flight, "I'm sure we'll come directly to Morva."

"Well done!" cried the bard. "I must say I never would have noticed it."

"That's at least one clever thing you've done today," Eilonwy admitted.

"This is not my doing," Taran said with a puzzled frown. "Adaon spoke the truth. His gift is a precious one." He told Eilonwy hurriedly about the clasp and the dreams of the night before.

"Don't you see?" he cried. "I dreamed about Fflewddur's harp—and we found Fflewddur himself. It wasn't all my own idea to go looking for a stream; it just came to me and I knew we would find it. Just now, when I saw the bird—that was in my dream. And there was another dream, a terrible one, of wolves. . . . That's going to happen, too. I'm sure of it. Adaon's dreams were always true. He told me of them."

At first Eilonwy was loath to believe him. "Adaon was a wonderful man," she said. "You can't tell me it was all because of a piece of iron. I don't care how magical it is."

"I don't mean that," Taran said. "What I believe," he added thoughtfully, "is that Adaon understood these things anyway. Even with his clasp, there is much I do not understand. All I know is that I *feel* differently somehow. I can see things I never saw before—or smell or taste them. I can't say exactly what it is. It's strange, and awesome in a way. And very beautiful sometimes. There are things that I know . . ." Taran shook his head. "And I don't even know how I know them."

Eilonwy was silent for a moment. "Yes," she said slowly, "I believe it now. You don't even sound quite like yourself. Adaon's clasp is a priceless gift. It gives you a kind of wisdom," she added, "which, I suppose, is what Assistant Pig-Keepers need more than anything else."

CHAPTER TEN

The Marshes of Morva

From the moment the marsh bird appeared, Taran led the companions swiftly, following without hesitation a path which now seemed clear. He felt the powerful muscles of Melynlas moving beneath him, and guided the steed with unaccustomed skill. The stallion responded to this new touch on the reins with mighty bursts of speed, so much so that Lluagor could barely keep pace. Fflewddur shouted for Taran to halt a bit and let them all catch their breath. Gurgi, looking like a windblown haystack, gratefully clambered down, and even Eilonwy gave a sigh of relief.

"Since we've stopped," Taran said, "Gurgi might as well share out some food. But we'd better find shelter first, if we don't want to get soaked."

"Soaked?" cried Fflewddur. "Great Belin, there isn't a cloud in the sky! It's a gorgeous day—taking everything into consideration."

"If I were you," Eilonwy advised the puzzled bard, "I should listen to him. Usually, that's not a wise thing to do. But the circumstances are a little different now."

The bard shrugged and shook his head, but followed Taran across the rolling fields into a shallow ravine. There, they found a wide and fairly deep recess in the shoulder of a hill.

"I hope you aren't wounded," remarked Fflewddur. "My war-leader at home has an old wound that gives him a twinge when the weather changes. Very handy, I admit; though it does seem a painful way of foretelling rain. I always think it's easier just to wait, and every kind of weather's bound to come along sooner or later."

"The wind has shifted," Taran said. "It comes from the sea now. It's restless, with a briny taste. There's a smell of grass and weeds, too, which makes me think we aren't far from Morva. If all goes well, we may reach the Marshes by tomorrow."

Soon afterward, the sky indeed clouded over and a chill rain began pelting against the hill. In moments it grew to a heavy downpour. Water coursed in rivulets on either side of their shelter, but the companions remained dry.

"Wise master," shouted Gurgi, "protects us from slippings and drippings!"

"I must say," the bard remarked, "you foretold it exactly."

"Not I," said Taran. "Without Adaon's clasp, I'm afraid we'd all have been drenched."

"How's that?" asked the perplexed Fflewddur. "I shouldn't think a clasp would have anything to do with it."

As he had explained to Eilonwy, Taran now told the bard what he had learned of the brooch. Fflewddur cautiously examined the ornament at Taran's throat.

"Very interesting," he said. "Whatever else it may have, it bears the bardic symbol—those three lines there, like a sort of arrowhead."

"I saw them," Taran said, "but I didn't know what they were."

"Naturally," said Fflewddur. "It's part of the secret lore of the bards. I learned that much when I was trying to study for my examinations."

"But what do they mean?" Taran asked.

"As I recall," put in Eilonwy, "the last time I asked him to read an inscription . . ."

"Yes," said Fflewddur with embarrassment, "that was something else again. But I know the bardic symbol well. It is secret, though since you have the clasp I don't suppose it can do any harm for me to tell you. The lines mean knowledge, truth, and love."

"That's very nice," said Eilonwy, "but I can't imagine why knowledge, truth, and love should be so much of a secret."

"Perhaps I should say unusual as much as secret," answered the bard. "I sometimes think it's hard enough to find any one of them, even separately. Put them all together and you have something very powerful indeed."

Taran, who had been thoughtfully fingering the clasp, stopped and looked about him uneasily. "Hurry," he said, "we must leave here at once."

"Taran of Caer Dallben," Eilonwy cried, "you're going too far! I can understand coming *out* of the rain, but I don't see deliberately going *into* it."

Nevertheless, she followed; and the companions, at Taran's urgent command, untethered the horses and ran from the hillside. They had not gone ten paces before the entire slope, weakened by the downpour, collapsed with a loud roar.

Gurgi yelped in terror and threw himself at Taran's feet. "Oh, great, brave, and wise master! Gurgi is thankful! His poor tender head is spared from terrible dashings and crashings!"

Fflewddur put his hands on his hips and gave a low whistle. "Well, well, fancy that. Another moment and we'd have been buried for good and all. Never part with that clasp, my friend. It's a true treasure."

Taran was silent. His hand went to Adaon's brooch, and he stared at the shattered hill slope with a look of wonder.

The rain slackened a little before nightfall. Although drenched and chilled to the bone, the companions had made good progress by the time Taran allowed them to rest again. Here, gray and cheerless moors spread before them. Wind and water had worn crevices in the earth, like the gougings of a giant's fingers. The companions made their camp in a narrow gorge, glad for the chance to sleep even on the muddy ground. Taran drowsed with one hand on the iron brooch, the other grasping his sword. He was less weary than he had expected, despite the grueling ride. A strange sense of excitement thrilled him, different from what he had felt when Dallben had presented him with the sword. However, his dreams that night were troubled and unhappy.

At first light, as the companions began their journey again, Taran spoke of his dreams to Eilonwy. "I can make no sense of them," he said with hesitation. "I saw Ellidyr in mortal danger. At the same time it was as though my hands were bound and I could not help him."

"I'm afraid the only place you're going to see Ellidyr is in your dreams," replied Eilonwy. "There certainly hasn't been a trace of him anywhere. For all we know, he could have been to Morva and gone, or not even reached the Marshes in the first place. It's too bad you didn't dream of an easier way to find that cauldron and put an end to all this. I'm cold and wet and at this point I'm beginning not to care who has it."

"I dreamed of the cauldron, too," Taran said anxiously. "But everything was confused and clouded. It seems to me we came upon the cauldron. And yet," he added, "when we found it, I wept."

Eilonwy, for once, was silent, and Taran had no heart to speak of the dream again.

Shortly after midday they reached the Marshes of Morva.

Taran had sensed them long before, as the ground had begun to turn spongy and treacherous under the hooves of Melynlas. He had seen more marsh birds and had heard, far in the distance, the weird and lonely voice of a loon. Ropes of fog, twisting and creeping like white serpents, had begun to rise from the reeking ground.

Now the companions halted, and stood in silence at a narrow neck of the swamp. From there, the Marshes of Morva stretched westward to the horizon. Here, huge growths of thorny furze rose up. At the far side, Taran distinguished meager clumps of wasted trees. Under the gray sky, pools of stagnant water flickered among dead grasses and broken reeds. A scent of ancient decay choked his nostrils. A ceaseless thrumming and groaning trembled in the air. Gurgi's eyes were round with terror, and the bard shifted uneasily on Lluagor.

"You've led us here well enough," said Eilonwy. "But how do you ever expect to go about finding a cauldron in a place like this?"

Taran motioned her to be silent. As he looked across the dreaded Marshes, something stirred in his mind. "Do not move," he cautioned in a low voice. He glanced quickly behind him. Gray shapes appeared from the line of bushes straggling over a hillock. They were not two wolves, as he had thought at first, but two Huntsmen in jackets of wolf pelts. Another Huntsman, in a heavy cloak of bearskin, crouched beside them.

"The Huntsmen have found us," Taran went on quickly. "Follow every step I take. But not a motion until I give the signal." Now he understood the dream of the wolves clearly, and knew exactly what he must do.

The Huntsmen, believing they could take their prey unawares, drew closer.

"Now!" shouted Taran. He urged Melynlas forward and galloped headlong into the Marshes. Heaving and plunging, the stallion labored through the mire. With a great shout, the Huntsmen raced after him. Once, Melynlas nearly foundered in a deep pool. The great strides of the pursuers brought them closer, so close that in a fearful backward glance Taran saw one of them, teeth bared in a snarl, reach out to clutch the stirrups of Lluagor.

Taran spun Melynlas to the right. Lluagor followed. A shout of terror rose behind them. One of the men clad in wolfskin had stumbled and pitched forward, screaming as the black bog seized and sucked him down. His two comrades grappled each other, striving desperately to flee the ground that fell away under their feet. The Huntsman in bearskin flung out his arms and scrabbled at the weeds, growling in rage; the last warrior trampled the sinking man, vainly seeking a foothold to escape the deadly bog.

Melynlas galloped onward. Brackish water spurted at his hooves, but Taran guided the powerful stallion along what seemed a chain of submerged islands, never stopping even when he reached the far side of the swamp. There, on more solid ground, he raced through the furze and beyond the clump of trees. While Lluagor pounded after him, Taran followed a long gully toward the protection of a high mound.

Suddenly he reined in the stallion. At the side of the mound, almost a part of the turf itself, rose a low cottage. It was so cleverly concealed with sod and branches that Taran had to look again to see there was a doorway. Circling the hill were tumbledown stables and something resembling a demolished chicken roost.

Taran began to back Melynlas away from this strange cluster of buildings and cautioned the others to keep silent.

"I shouldn't worry about that," Eilonwy said. "Whoever lives in there surely heard us coming. If they aren't out to welcome us or fight with us by now, then I don't think anyone's there at all." She leaped from Melynlas and made her way toward the cottage.

"Come back!" Taran called. He unsheathed his sword and followed her. The bard and Gurgi dismounted and drew their own weapons.

Alert and cautious, Taran approached the low doorway. Eilonwy had discovered a window, half-hidden by turf and grass, and was peering through it. "I don't see anybody," she said, as the others came up beside her. "Look for yourself."

"For the matter of that," said the bard, ducking his head and squinting past Eilonwy, "I don't think anyone's been here for quite some time. So much the better! In any case, we'll have a dry place to rest."

The chamber, Taran saw, indeed seemed deserted, of inhabitants, at least, for the room was even more heaped up and disorderly than Dallben's. In one corner stood a wide loom with a good many of the threads straggling down. The work on the frame was less than half-finished and so tangled and knotted he could imagine no one ever continuing it. Broken crockery covered a small table. Rusted and broken weapons were piled about.

"How would you like it," asked a cheerful voice behind Taran, "if you were turned into a toad? And stepped on?"

CHAPTER ELEVEN

The Cottage

Taran spun around and raised his sword. Suddenly in his hand writhed a cold serpent, hissing and twisting to strike. With a cry of horror he flung it away. The serpent fell to the ground, and there, in its place, lay Taran's blade. Eilonwy stifled a scream. Taran drew back fearfully.

Facing him was a short and rather plump little woman with a round, lumpy face and a pair of very sharp black eyes. Her hair hung like a clump of discolored marsh weeds, bound with vines and ornamented with bejeweled pins that seemed about to lose themselves in the hopeless tangle. She wore a dark, shapeless, ungirt robe covered with patches and stains. Her feet were bare and exceptionally large.

The companions drew closer together. Gurgi, trembling violently, crouched behind Taran. The bard, looking pale and uneasy, nevertheless prepared to stand his ground.

"Come along, my ducklings," the enchantress said cheerily. "I promise it won't hurt a bit. You can bring your sword if you want," she added with an indulgent smile at Taran, "though you won't need it. I've never seen a toad with a sword. On the other hand, I've never seen a sword with a toad, so you're welcome to do as you please."

"We please to stay as we are," cried Eilonwy. "Don't think we're going to let anybody . . ."

"Who are you?" Taran cried. "We have done you no harm. You have no cause to threaten us."

"How many twigs in a bird's nest?" asked the enchantress suddenly. "Answer quickly. There, you see," she added. "Poor chicks, you don't even know that. How could you be expected to know what you really want out of life?"

"One thing I want," retorted Eilonwy, "is not to be a toad."

"You're a pretty little duck," said the enchantress in a kind, cajoling voice. "Would you give me your hair once you've done with it? I have such trouble with mine these days. Do you ever have the feeling things are disappearing into it and you might never see them again?

"No matter," she went on. "You'll enjoy being toads, skipping about here and there, sitting on toadstools—well, perhaps not that. Toads don't really sit on toadstools. But you might dance in dew circles. Now there's a charming thought.

"Don't be frightened," she added, leaning over and whispering in Taran's ear. "You can't for a moment imagine I'd do all I said. Goodness no, I wouldn't dream of stepping on you. I couldn't stand the squashiness."

With mounting terror, Taran cast desperately about in his mind for some means of saving his companions. He would have considered this disheveled creature's intention as mad and impossible had he not remembered the serpent in his hand, its menacing fangs and cold eyes.

"You mightn't like being toads at first," the enchantress said reasonably. "It takes getting used to. But," she added in a reassuring tone, "once it's happened, I'm certain you wouldn't want it any other way."

"Why are you doing this?" Taran cried with all the more anger at feeling himself powerless. He turned his head in fear and revulsion as the enchantress gave him a kindly pat on the cheek.

"Can't have people poking and prying," she said. "You understand that much, don't you? Make an exception for one, then it's two, three, and next thing you know, hundreds and hundreds trampling things and getting underfoot. Believe me, this is best for everybody."

From around the side of the hill, at that moment, two more figures appeared. Both closely resembled the stout little woman, except that one wore a black cloak with the hood pulled up, nearly concealing her face; and at the throat of the other hung a necklace of milky white stones.

The enchantress ran to them and called out happily, "Orwen! Orgoch! Hurry! We're going to make toads!"

Taran gasped. He shot a quick glance at the bard and Eilonwy. "Did you hear those names?" he whispered hurriedly. "We've found them!"

The bard's face was filled with alarm. "Much good it may do us," he said. "By the time they're through, I don't think we're going to care about the cauldron or anything else. I've never danced in a dew circle," he continued under his breath. "In different circumstances I might enjoy it. But not now," he added with a shudder.

"I've never met a person," whispered Eilonwy, while Gurgi snuffled in fright, "who could talk about such dreadful things and smile at the same time. It's like ants walking up and down your back."

"We must try to take them unawares," Taran said. "I don't know what they can do to all of us all at once. I don't even know if there's anything we can do to them. But we must take the chance. One or two of us may survive."

"I suppose that's all we can do," agreed the bard. He swallowed with difficulty and gave Taran a worried look. "If it should turn out that I—I mean, if I should be—yes, well, what I mean is should anything happen to me, I beg you, do pay attention to where you tread."

Meantime, the three enchantresses had returned to the cottage. "Oh, Orddu," the one with the necklace was saying, "why must it always be toads? Can't you think of anything else?"

"But they're so neat," replied Orddu, "compact and convenient."

"What's wrong with toads?" asked the hooded one. "That's the trouble with you, Orwen, always trying to make things complicated."

"I only suggested something else, Orgoch," answered the enchant-ress called Orwen, "for the sake of variety."

"I love toads," murmured Orgoch, smacking her lips. Even in the shadow of the hood Taran could see the features of the enchantress moving and twitching in what he feared was impatience.

"Look at them standing there," Orddu said, "poor little goslings, all wet and muddy. I've been talking to them, and I think they finally realize what's best for them."

"Why, those are the ones we saw galloping across the Marsh," said Orwen, toying with her beads. "It was so clever of you," she added, smiling at Taran, "to have the Huntsmen swallowed up in the bog, really quite well done."

"Disgusting creatures, Huntsmen," muttered Orgoch. "Nasty, hairy, vicious things. They turn my stomach."

"They stick to their work," ventured the bard. "I'll say that much for them."

"We had a whole flock of Huntsmen here the other day," said Orddu. "They were poking and prying around, just as you were. Now you understand why I said we couldn't make exceptions."

"We didn't make exceptions of *them*, did we, Orddu?" said Orwen. "Though it wasn't toads, if you remember."

"I remember very distinctly, my dear," replied the first enchantress, "but you were Orddu then. And when you're being Orddu, you can do as you please. But I'm Orddu today, and what I say is . . ."

"That's not fair," interrupted Orgoch. "You always want to be Orddu. I've had to be Orgoch three times in a row, while you've only been Orgoch once."

"It's not our fault, my sweet," said Orddu, "if we don't like being Orgoch. It isn't comfortable, you know. You have such horrid indigestion. If you'd only pay more attention to what you take for your meals."

Taran had been trying to follow this conversation of the enchantresses, but found himself more confused than ever. Now he had no clear idea which was really Orddu, Orwen, and Orgoch, or whether they were all three the same. However, their remarks about the Huntsmen gave him hope for the first time.

"If the Huntsmen of Annuvin are your enemies," Taran said, "then we have common cause. We, too, have fought against them."

"Enemies, friends, it all comes to the same in the end," muttered Orgoch. "Do make haste, Orddu, and take them off to the shed. It's been a terribly long morning."

"You are a greedy creature," said Orddu, with a tolerant smile at the hooded crone. "There's another reason why neither of us wants to be Orgoch if we can possibly help it. Perhaps if you learned to control yourself better . . . ? Now listen to what these dear mice have to tell us. It should be interesting; they say such charming things."

Orddu turned to Taran. "Now, my duckling," she said pleasantly, "how did it come about that you're on such bad terms with the Huntsmen?"

Taran hesitated, fearful of revealing Gwydion's plan. "They attacked us," he began.

"Of course they did, my poor goslings," said Orddu with sympathy. "They're always attacking everybody. That's one of the advantages of being toads; you needn't worry about such things any more. It will be all romps in the forest and lovely wet mornings. The Huntsmen won't vex you any more. True, you shall have to keep an eye out for herons, kingfishers, and serpents. But apart from that, you won't have a care in the world."

"But who is 'us'?" interrupted Orwen. She turned to Orddu. "Aren't you going to find out their names?"

"Yes, by all means," murmured Orgoch, with a lip-smacking sound. "I love names."

Once again Taran hesitated. "This . . . this," he said gesturing toward Eilonwy, "is Indeg. And Prince Glessic . . ."

Orwen giggled and gave Orddu an affectionate nudge. "Listen to them," she said. "They're delightful when they lie."

"If they won't give their right names," said Orgoch, "then simply take them."

Taran stopped short. Orddu was studying him closely. With sudden discouragement, he realized his efforts were useless. "This is Eilonwy Daughter of Angharad," he said. "And Fflewddur Fflam."

"A bard of the harp," Fflewddur added.

"And this is Gurgi," Taran continued.

"So that's a gurgi," said Orwen with great interest. "It seems to me I've heard of them, but I never knew what they were."

"It's not *a* gurgi," retorted Eilonwy. "It's Gurgi. And there's only one."

"Yes, yes!" Gurgi put in, venturing to step from behind Taran. "And he is bold and clever! He will not let brave companions become toads with humpings and jumpings!"

Orgoch looked curiously at him. "What do you do with the gurgi?" she asked. "Do you eat it or sit on it?"

"I should think," Orddu suggested, "whatever you did, you would have to clean it first. And you, my duck," she said to Taran, "who are you?"

Taran straightened and threw back his head. "I am Taran," he said, "Assistant Pig-Keeper of Caer Dallben."

"Dallben!" cried Orddu. "You poor lost chicken, why didn't you say so in the first place? Tell me, how is dear little Dallben?"

CHAPTER TWELVE

Little Dallben

Taran's jaw dropped. Before he could answer, the enchant-resses had crowded around the companions and were lead-ing them to the cottage. In wonder, he turned to Fflewddur, who looked less pale now that Orddu had stopped speaking of toads.

"*Little* Dallben?" Taran whispered. "I've never in my life heard anyone talk about him that way. Can they mean the same Dallben?"

"I don't know," whispered the bard in return. "But if they think it is—Great Belin, don't tell them otherwise!"

Inside, with a great deal of joyous bustling that in fact accom-plished little, the enchantresses hurried to straighten up the cham-ber. Orwen, in obvious excitement and delight, brought out a number of rickety chairs and stools; Orgoch cleared the table of crockery by brushing it onto the floor; Orddu clapped her hands and beamed at the companions.

"I should never have thought it," she began. "Oh, no, no, my duck!" she cried suddenly to Eilonwy, who had drawn closer to the loom and had just bent forward to examine the fabric. "Mustn't touch. Nasty prickles if you do. It's full of nettles. Come sit with us, there's a love."

Despite the sudden warmth of their welcome, Taran glanced at the enchantresses with uneasiness. The chamber itself filled him with odd forebodings he could not name, which eluded him like shadows. Gurgi and the bard, however, appeared delighted at the strange turn of events, and set heartily to eating the food that soon arrived at the table. Taran looked questioningly at Eilonwy.

The girl guessed his thought. "Don't be afraid to eat," she said behind her hand. "It's perfectly all right, not the least bit poisonous or enchanted. I can tell. I learned how when I was staying with Queen Achren and learning to be a sorceress. What you do is . . ."

"Now, my sparrow," Orddu interrupted, "you must tell us all about dear little Dallben. What is he doing? Does he still have *The Book of Three?*"

"Well . . . why, yes he does," Taran said, with some confusion, beginning to wonder if the enchantresses did not know more about Dallben than he did.

"Poor little robin," remarked Orddu, "and such a heavy book. I'm surprised he would even be able to turn the pages."

"Well, you see," Taran said, still puzzled, "the Dallben that we know, he isn't little. I mean, he's rather elderly."

"Elderly!" burst out Fflewddur. "He's every bit of three hundred and eighty years old! Coll himself told me."

"He was such a dear, sweet little thing," said Orwen with a sigh. "All pink cheeks and chubby fingers."

"I love babies," said Orgoch, smacking her lips.

"His hair is quite gray," said Taran, who could not bring himself to believe these strange creatures were indeed speaking of his old teacher. The idea of the learned Dallben ever having pink cheeks and chubby fingers was beyond his imagination. "He has a beard too," he added.

"A beard?" cried Orddu. "What's little Dallben doing with a

beard? Why in the world should he want such a thing? Such a charming little tadpole!"

"We found him in the marsh one morning," said Orwen. "All by himself in a great wicker basket. It was too sweet for words. Orgoch, of course . . ."

At this Orgoch made an irritable noise and her eyes glared from the depths of the hood.

"Come now, dear Orgoch, don't look so disagreeable," said Orddu. "We're all friends together here; we can talk about such things now. Well, I shall put it this way and spare Orgoch's feelings. She didn't want to keep him. That is, not in the usual sense. But we did. And so we brought the poor fledgling to the cottage."

"He grew very quickly," added Orwen. "Why, it was no time before he was toddling around, and talking, and doing little errands. So kind and polite. A perfect joy. And you say he has a beard?" She shook her head. "Curious notion. Wherever did he find it?"

"Yes, a delightful little sparrow he was," said Orddu. "But then," she continued with a sad smile, "there was that distressing accident. We were brewing some herbs one morning, a rather special potion."

"And Dallben," sighed Orwen, "sweet little Dallben was stirring the kettle for us. It was one of those kind, thoughtful things he was always doing. But when it came to a boil, some of it bubbled up and splashed out."

"It burned his poor dear fingers," Orddu added. "But he didn't cry, no indeed. He just popped his fingers into his mouth, the brave little starling. Of course, some of the potion was still there, and he swallowed it."

"As soon as he did that," explained Orwen, "he knew every bit as much as we did. It was a magical brew, you understand, a recipe for wisdom."

"After that," Orddu went on, "it was out of the question to keep him with us. It would never have been the same; no, it would never have done at all; you can't have that many people knowing that much all under the same roof. Especially since he was able to guess some of the things Orgoch had in mind. And so we had to let him go—really let him go, that is. Orgoch, by this time, was the one who wanted to keep him. In her own fashion, which I doubt he would have liked."

"He would have been a sweet little thing," murmured Orgoch.

"I must say we did quite handsomely by him," Orddu continued. "We gave him his choice of a harp, a sword, or *The Book of Three*. Had he chosen the harp, he could have been the greatest bard in the world; the sword and the dear duckling could have ruled all Prydain. But," Orddu said, "he chose *The Book of Three*. And to tell the truth, we were just as happy that he did, for it was heavy and moldy and did nothing but gather dust. And so he left to make his way in the world. And that was the last we saw of him."

"A good thing sweet, dear Dallben isn't here," Fflewddur chuckled to Taran. "Their description hardly matches. I fear they might be rather startled."

Taran had been silent throughout Orddu's account, wondering how he dared bring up the matter of the cauldron. "Dallben has been my master as long as I can remember," he said at last, deciding frankness was the best way to go about it—especially since the enchantresses seemed able to guess when he was not telling the truth. "If you are as fond of him as I . . ."

"We love him dearly, the sweet thing," said Orddu, "you can be sure of that."

"Then I beg you to help us carry out his wishes and the wishes of Gwydion Prince of Don," Taran went on. He explained what had taken place at the council, what they had learned at Dark Gate and from Gwystyl. He spoke of the urgency of bringing the cauldron to Caer Dallben, and asked, too, whether the enchantresses had seen Ellidyr.

Orddu shook her head. "A Son of Pen-Llarcau? No, my duck, there's been no such person anywhere near. If he'd come across the Marshes, we'd have been bound to see him."

"We have a lovely view of the fens from the hilltop," Orwen put in with such enthusiasm that her necklace bounced and rattled. "You must come and enjoy it. Indeed, you're perfectly welcome to stay as long as you want," she added eagerly. "Now that little Dallben's gone, and found himself a beard, too, the place isn't half as cheery as it used to be. We wouldn't change you into a toad— unless you insisted on it."

"Stay, by all means," croaked Orgoch with a leer.

"Our task is to regain the cauldron," Taran pressed, preferring to overlook Orgoch's remark. "From what Gwystyl told us . . ."

"You said his crow told you, my lamb," interrupted Orddu. "Don't believe everything you hear from a crow."

"Doli of the Fair Folk believed him," Taran said. "Do you tell me now that you have no cauldron? I ask you this in the name of Dallben himself."

"Cauldron?" answered Orddu. "Why, goodness, we have dozens! Cauldrons, kettles, cook-pots—we can hardly keep track of them all."

"I speak of the cauldron of Annuvin," Taran said firmly, "the cauldron of Arawn and his deathless warriors."

"Oh," said Orddu, laughing cheerfully, "you must mean the Black Crochan."

"I do not know its name," Taran said, "but that may be the one we seek."

"Are you sure you wouldn't prefer one of the others?" asked Orwen. "They're much more attractive than that old thing. And much more practical. What use have you for Cauldron-Born? They would only be a nuisance. We can give you a kettle to brew the most marvelous sleeping potions, or one you can sprinkle on daffodils to take away that bilious yellow."

"Our concern is with the Black Crochan," Taran insisted, deciding this was indeed the name of Arawn's cauldron. "Will you not tell me the truth? Is the cauldron here?"

"Of course it's here," replied Orddu. "Why not, since it was ours to begin with? And always has been!"

"Yours?" cried Taran. "Then Arawn stole it from you?"

"Stole?" Orddu answered. "Not exactly. No, we couldn't say it was stolen."

"But you couldn't have given it to Arawn," Eilonwy cried, "knowing what he meant to use it for!"

"Even Arawn had to be allowed to have his chance," said Orddu tolerantly. "One day you'll understand why. For there is a destiny laid on everything; on big, ugly Crochans as well as poor little ducklings, and a destiny laid even on us. Besides, Arawn paid dearly for the use of it, very dearly indeed, you can be sure. The details, my duckling, are of a private nature which does not concern you. In any case, the Crochan was not to be his forever."

"Arawn swore to return it after a time," said Orwen. "But when the time came, he broke his oath to us, as might be expected."

"Ill-advised," murmured Orgoch.

"And since he wouldn't give it back," Orddu said, "what else could we do? We went and took it."

"Great Belin!" cried the bard. "You three ladies ventured into the heart of Annuvin and carried the thing out? How did you ever manage?"

Orddu smiled. "There are a number of ways, my curious sparrow. We could have flooded Annuvin with darkness and floated the cauldron out. We could have put all the guards to sleep. Or we could have turned ourselves into—well, no matter—let us say we could have used a variety of methods. In any case, the cauldron is here again.

"And," the enchantress added, "here it will stay. No, no," she said, raising a hand to Taran. "I can see you'd like to have it, but that's out of the question. Much too dangerous for wandering chicks like you. My goodness, we shouldn't sleep at night. No, no, not even for the sake of little Dallben.

"In fact," Orddu went on, "you'd be much safer being toads than having anything to do with the Black Crochan." She shook her head. "Better yet, we could change you into birds and have you fly back to Caer Dallben immediately.

"No indeed," she continued, rising from the table and taking hold of Taran's shoulders. "Off you ducklings must go and never give a second thought to the Crochan. Tell dear little Dallben and Prince Gwydion we're terribly sorry, and if there's anything else we can possibly do . . . But not that. Oh, my, no."

Taran started to protest, but Orddu cut him short and guided him rapidly to the door, while the other enchantresses hustled the companions after him.

"You may sleep in the shed tonight, my chickens," said Orddu. "Then, first thing in the morning, away with you to little Dallben. And you shall decide whether you'd rather go on your legs. Or," she added, this time without a smile, "on a pair of your own wings."

"Or," muttered Orgoch, "hopping all the way."

CHAPTER THIRTEEN

The Plan

The door slammed shut behind them and once again the companions found themselves outside the cottage.

"Well, I like that!" Eilonwy cried indignantly. "After all their talk of dear little Dallben and sweet little Dallben, they've turned us out!"

"Better turned *out* than *into*, if you take my meaning," said the bard. "A Fflam is always kind to animals, but somehow I can't bring myself to feel I should like to actually become one!"

"No, oh, no!" Gurgi cried fervently. "Gurgi, too, wants to stay as he is—bold and clever!"

Taran turned back to the cottage and began pounding on the door. "They must listen to us!" he declared. "They didn't even take time to think it over." But the door did not open, and though he ran to the window and rapped long and loud, the enchantresses did not show themselves again.

"I'm afraid that's your answer," said Fflewddur. "They've said all they intend to say—and perhaps it's for the best. And I have the uneasy feeling all that knocking and thumping might— well, you don't know but what those, ah, ladies get upset at noises."

"We can't just go away," Taran replied. "The cauldron is in their hands and, friends of Dallben or not, there's no telling what they'll do with it. I fear them and I distrust them. You heard the way the one called Orgoch was talking. Yes, I can well imagine what she'd have done to Dallben." He shook his head gravely. "This is what Gwydion warned against. Whoever has the cauldron can be a mortal threat to Prydain, if they choose to be."

"At least Ellidyr hasn't found it," Eilonwy said. "That's something to be grateful for."

"If you want the advice of one who is, after all, the oldest of us here," said the bard, "I think we should do well to hurry home and let Dallben and Gwydion attend to the matter. After all, Dallben should know how to deal with those three."

"No," Taran answered, "that I will not do. We should lose precious days in travel. The Huntsmen failed to get the cauldron back. But who knows what Arawn will attempt next? No, we dare not leave the thing here."

"For once," declared Eilonwy, "I agree. We've come this far and we shall have to go on to the end. I don't trust those enchantresses either. *They* wouldn't sleep if they thought we had the cauldron? I shall certainly have nightmares if I think of *them* with it! Not to mention Arawn! I believe no one, human or otherwise, should have that much power." She shuddered. "Ugh! There go the ants on my back again!"

"Yes, well, it's true," Fflewddur began. "But the fact remains— they have that wretched pot and we don't. They're *there* and we're *here*, and it looks very much as though it will stay that way."

Taran was thoughtful a moment. "When Arawn wouldn't give the cauldron back to them," he said, "they went and took it. Now, since they won't let us have the cauldron, I see only one way: *we* shall have to take it."

"Steal it?" cried the bard. His worried expression changed rapidly and his eyes brightened. "I mean," he dropped his voice to a whisper, "steal it? Now there's a thought," he went on eagerly. "Never occurred to me. Yes, yes, that's the way," he added with excitement. "Now, that has some style and flair to it!"

"One difficulty," Eilonwy said. "We don't know where they've hidden the cauldron, and they evidently aren't going to let us in to find out."

Taran frowned. "I wish Doli were here; we'd have no trouble at all. I don't know—there must be some way. They told us we could stay the night," he continued. "That gives us from now until dawn. Come, let's not stand in front of their cottage or they'll know we're up to something. Orddu spoke of a shed."

The companions led their horses to the side of the hill where a low, dilapidated building tottered shakily on the turf. It was bare and bleak and the autumn wind whistled through the chinks in the earthen wall. The bard stamped his feet and beat his arms.

"Chilly spot to plan anything," he remarked. "Those enchantresses may have a lovely view of the Marshes, but it's a cold one."

"I wish we had some straw," Eilonwy said, "or anything to keep us warm. We'll freeze before we have a chance to think of anything at all."

"Gurgi will find straw," Gurgi suggested. He scurried out of the shed and ran toward the chicken roost.

Taran paced back and forth. "We'll have to get into the cottage as soon as they're asleep." He shook his head and fingered the brooch at his throat. "But how? Adaon's clasp has given me no idea. The dreams I had of the cauldron are without meaning to me. If I could only understand them . . ."

"Suppose you dozed off right now," said Fflewddur helpfully, "and slept as fast as you could? As hard as you could, I mean. You might find the answer."

"I'm not sure," replied Taran. "It doesn't quite work that way."

"It should be a lot easier than boring a hole through the hill," said the bard, "which was my next suggestion."

"We could block up their chimney and smoke them out," Eilonwy said. "Then one of us could sneak into the cottage. No," she added, "on second thought, I'm afraid anything we might put *down* their chimney—well—they could very likely put something worse *up*. Besides, they don't have a chimney, so we shall have to forget that idea."

Gurgi, meantime, had returned with a huge armload of straw from the chicken roost, and the companions gratefully began heaping it on the clay floor. While Gurgi went off again to fetch another load, Taran looked dubiously at the straggly pile.

"I suppose I could try to dream," he said, without much hope. "I certainly haven't a better suggestion."

"We can bed you down very nicely," said Fflewddur, "and while you're dreaming, the rest of us will be thinking, too. That way, we can all be working after our own fashion. I don't mind telling you," he added, "I wish I had Adaon's brooch. Sleep? I wouldn't need to be asked twice, for I'm weary to my bones."

Taran, still unsure, made ready to settle himself in the straw when Gurgi reappeared, wide-eyed and trembling. The creature was so upset he could only gasp and gesture. Taran sprang to his feet. "What is it?" he cried.

Gurgi beckoned them toward the chicken roost and the companions hurried after him. The agitated Gurgi led them into the wattle-and-daub building, then slunk back, terrified. He pointed to the far corner. There, in the midst of the straw, stood a cauldron.

It was squat and black, and half as tall as a man. Its ugly mouth gaped wide enough to hold a human body. The rim of the cauldron was crooked and battered, its sides dented and scarred; on its lips and on the curve of its belly lay dark brown flecks and stains which Taran knew were not rust. A long, thick handle was braced by a heavy bar; two heavy rings, like the links of a great chain, were set in either side. Though of iron, the cauldron seemed alive, grim and brooding with ancient evil. The empty mouth caught the chill breeze and a hushed muttering rose from the cauldron's depths, like the lost voices of the tormented dead.

"It is the Black Crochan," Taran whispered in fear and awe. He well understood Gurgi's terror, for the very sight of the cauldron was enough to make him feel an icy hand clutching his heart. He turned away, hardly daring to look at it any longer.

Fflewddur's face was pale. Eilonwy put a hand to her mouth. In the corner, Gurgi shivered pitifully. Though he himself had found it, he gave no joyous yelps of triumph. Instead, he sank deeper into the straw and tried to make himself as small as possible.

"Yes, well, I suppose it is indeed," replied Fflewddur, swallowing hard. "On the other hand," he added hopefully, "perhaps it is not. They did say they had a number of other cauldrons and kettles lying about. I mean, we shouldn't want to make a mistake."

"It is the Crochan," Taran said. "I have dreamed of it. And even if I had not, I would know it still, for I can sense the evil in it."

"I, too," murmured Eilonwy. "It is full of death and suffering. I understand why Gwydion wants to destroy it." She turned to

Taran. "You were right in seeking it without delay," Eilonwy added with a shudder. "I'll take back all the things I said. The Crochan must be destroyed as soon as possible."

"Yes," Fflewddur sighed, "I'm afraid this is the Crochan itself. Why couldn't it have been a nice little kettle instead of this ugly, hulking brute? However," he went on, taking a deep breath, "let's snatch it! A Fflam never hesitates!"

"No!" cried Taran, putting out a hand to restrain the bard. "We dare not take it in broad daylight; and we mustn't stay here or they'll know we've found it. We'll come back after nightfall with the horses and drag it away. For now, we'd better keep to the shed and act as if nothing has happened."

The companions quickly returned to the shed. Once away from the Crochan, Gurgi regained some of his spirits. "Crafty Gurgi found it!" he cried. "Oh, yes! He always finds what is lost! He has found piggies, and now he finds a great cauldron of wicked doings and brewings! Kind master will honor humble Gurgi!" Nevertheless, his face wrinkled with fear.

Taran gave Gurgi a comforting pat on the shoulder. "Yes, old friend," he said, "you have helped us more than once. But I never would have imagined they'd have hidden the Crochan in an empty chicken roost, under a pile of dirty straw." He shook his head. "I'd think they'd want to guard it better."

"Not at all," said the bard. "They were very clever. They put it in one of the first places anybody would look, knowing quite well it was so easy nobody would ever think of looking there."

"Perhaps," Taran said. He frowned. "Or perhaps," he added, unable to stifle the dread suddenly filling him, "they meant us to find it."

✤

In the shed the companions tried to sleep, knowing the night to come would be one of hard and dangerous labor. Fflewddur and Gurgi dozed briefly; Eilonwy huddled in her cloak with some straw piled around her. Taran was too restless and uneasy even to close his eyes. He sat silently, in his hands a long coil of rope he had taken from what little gear remained to the companions. They had decided to sling the cauldron between the two horses and make their way from the Marshes into the safe shelter of the forest, where they would destroy the Crochan.

No sign of life came from the cottage. At nightfall, however, a candle suddenly glowed in the window. Taran rose quietly and moved stealthily out of the shed. Clinging to the shadows, he made his way to the low building and peered in. For a moment he stood there, amazed, unable to move. Then he turned and raced back to the others as quickly as he could.

"I saw them in there!" he whispered, rousing the bard and Gurgi. "They aren't the same ones at all!"

"What?" cried Eilonwy. "Are you sure you didn't stumble on a different cottage?"

"Of course I didn't," retorted Taran. "And if you don't believe me, go and look for yourself. They aren't the same. There are three of them, yes, but they're different. One of them was carding wool; one of them was spinning; and the third was weaving."

"I suppose, really," said the bard, "it passes the time for them. There's little enough to do in the middle of these dismal bogs."

"I shall indeed have to see for myself," Eilonwy declared. "There's nothing so strange about weaving, but beyond that I can't make any sense of what you say."

With Taran leading, the companions stole cautiously to the window. It was as he had said. Inside the cottage three figures went about their tasks, but not one of them resembled Orddu, Orwen, or Orgoch.

"They're beautiful!" whispered Eilonwy.

"I've heard of hags trying to disguise themselves as beautiful maidens," murmured the bard, "but I've never heard of beautiful maidens wanting to disguise themselves as hags. It isn't natural, and I don't mind telling you it makes me edgy. I think we'd better seize the cauldron and be gone."

"I don't know who they are," said Taran, "but I fear they are more powerful than we could even guess. Somehow we've fallen on something—I don't know what. It troubles me. Yes, we must take the cauldron as soon as we can, but we shall wait until they're asleep."

"*If* they sleep," said the bard. "Now that I've seen this, nothing would surprise me, not even if they hung by their toes all night, like bats."

For a long time Taran feared the bard was right and that the enchantresses might not sleep at all. The companions took turns watching the cottage and it was not until almost dawn that the candle finally winked out. In an agony of waiting, Taran still delayed. Soon a loud snoring rose from within.

"They must have gone back to themselves again," remarked the bard. "I can't imagine beautiful ladies snoring like that. No, it's Orgoch. I'd recognize that snort anywhere."

In the still shadows of the false dawn the companions hastened to the chicken roost where Eilonwy ventured to light her bauble.

The Crochan squatted in its corner, black and baleful.

"Hurry now," Taran ordered, taking hold of the handle.

"Fflewddur and Eilonwy, pick up those rings; and Gurgi, lift the other side. We'll haul it out and rope it to the horses. Ready? All lift together."

The companions gave a mighty heave, then nearly fell to the ground. The cauldron had not moved.

"It's heavier than I thought," said Taran. "Try again." He made to shift his grip on the handle. But his hands would not come free. In a spurt of fear, he tried to pull away. It was in vain.

"I say," muttered the bard, "I seem to be caught on something."

"So am I!" Eilonwy cried, struggling to tear her hands loose.

"And Gurgi is caught!" howled the terrified Gurgi. "Oh, sorrow! He cannot move!"

Desperately the companions flung themselves back and forth, fighting against the mute, iron enemy. Taran wrenched and tugged until he sobbed for lack of strength. Eilonwy had dropped in exhaustion, her hands still on the heavy ring. Once again, Taran strained to break free. The Black Crochan held him fast.

A figure in a long night robe appeared at the doorway.

"It's Orddu!" cried the bard. "We'll be toads for sure!"

CHAPTER FOURTEEN

The Price

Orddu, blinking sleepily and looking more disheveled than ever, stepped inside the chicken roost. Behind her followed the other two enchantresses, also in flapping night robes, their hair unbound and falling about their shoulders in a mass of snarls and tangles. They had again taken the shapes of crones, in no way resembling the maidens Taran had spied through the window.

Orddu raised a sputtering candle above her head and peered at the companions.

"Oh, the poor lambs!" she cried. "What have they gone and done? We tried to warn them about the nasty Crochan, but the headstrong little goslings wouldn't listen! My, oh my," she clucked sorrowfully, "now they've got their little fingers caught!"

"Don't you think," said Orgoch in a croaking whisper, "we should start the fire?"

Orddu turned to her. "Do be silent, Orgoch," she cried. "What a dreadful thought. It's much too early for breakfast."

"Never too early," muttered Orgoch.

"Look at them," Orddu went on fondly. "They're so charming when they're frightened. Like birdlings without their feathers."

"You have tricked us, Orddu!" Taran cried. "You knew we'd find the cauldron and you knew what would happen!"

"Why, of course we did, my chicken," Orddu replied sweetly. "We were only curious to find out what you'd do when you did find it. And now you've found it, and now we know!"

Taran struggled desperately to free himself. Despite his terror, he flung back his head and glared defiantly at Orddu. "Kill us if you choose, you evil hags!" he cried. "Yes, we would have stolen the cauldron and destroyed it! And so shall I try again, as long as I live!" Taran threw himself furiously against the immovable Crochan and once again with all his strength tried vainly to wrest it from the ground.

"I love to see them get angry, don't you?" Orwen whispered happily to Orgoch.

"Do take care," Orddu advised Taran, "or you'll harm yourself with all that thrashing about. We forgive you for calling us hags," she added indulgently. "You're upset, poor chicken, and liable to say anything."

"You are evil creatures!" Taran cried. "Do with us what you will, but sooner or later you shall be overcome. Gwydion shall learn of our fate. And Dallben . . ."

"Yes, yes!" shouted Gurgi. "They will find you, oh, yes! With great fightings and smitings!"

"My dear pullets," replied Orddu, "you still don't understand, do you? Evil? Why, bless your little thumping hearts, we aren't evil."

"I should hardly call this 'good,'" muttered the bard. "Not, at least, from a personal point of view."

"Of course not," agreed Orddu. "We're neither good nor evil. We're simply interested in things as they are. And things as they are, at the moment, seem to be that you're caught by the Crochan."

"And you don't care!" cried Eilonwy. "That's worse than being evil!"

"Certainly we care, my dear," Orwen said soothingly. "It's that we don't care in quite the same way you do, or rather *care* isn't really a feeling we can have."

"Come now," said Orddu, "don't trouble your thoughts with such matters. We've been talking and talking and we have some pleasant news for you. Bring the Crochan outdoors—it's so stuffy and eggy in here—and we shall tell you. Go ahead," she added, "you can lift it now."

Taran cast Orddu a distrustful glance, but ventured to put his weight against the cauldron. It moved, and he discovered, too, his hands were free. With much labor the companions managed to raise the heavy Crochan and carry it from the chicken roost.

Outside, the sun had already risen. As the companions set the cauldron on the ground and quickly drew away, the rays of dawn turned the black iron as red as blood.

"Yes, now as I was saying," Orddu continued, while Taran and his companions rubbed their aching arms and hands, "we've talked it over and we agree—even Orgoch agrees—that you shall have the Crochan if you truly want it."

"You'll let us take it?" cried Taran. "After all you've done?"

"Quite so," replied Orddu. "The Crochan is useless—except for making Cauldron-Born. Arawn has spoiled it for anything else, as you might imagine. It's sad it should be so, but that's the way things are. Now, I assure you, Cauldron-Born are the last creatures in the world we should want around here. We've decided the Crochan is nothing but a bother to us. And, since you're friends of Dallben . . ."

"You're giving us the Crochan?" Taran began in astonishment.

"Delighted to oblige you ladies," said the bard.

"Gently, gently, my ducklings," Orddu interrupted. "*Give* you the Crochan? Oh, goodness no! We never *give* anything. Only what is worth earning is worth having. But we shall allow you the opportunity to buy it."

"We have no treasures to bargain with," Taran said in dismay. "Alas that we do not."

"We couldn't expect you to pay as much as Arawn did," replied Orddu, "but we're sure you can find something to offer in exchange. Oh, shall we say . . . the North Wind in a bag?"

"The North Wind!" Taran exclaimed. "Impossible! How could you ever dream. . . ?"

"Very well," said Orddu, "we shan't be difficult. The South Wind, then. It's much gentler."

"You make sport of us," Taran cried angrily. "The price you ask is beyond what any of us can pay."

Orddu hesitated. "Possibly you're right," she admitted. "Well, then, something a little more personal. I have it!" she said, beaming at Taran. "Give us—give us the nicest summer day you can remember! You can't say that's hard, since it belongs to you!"

"Yes," Orwen said eagerly. "A lovely summer afternoon full of sunlight and sleepy scents."

"There's nothing so sweet," murmured Orgoch, sucking a tooth, "as a tender young lamb's summer afternoon."

"How can I give you that?" protested Taran. "Or any other day, when they're—they're inside of me somewhere? You can't get them out! I mean . . ."

"We could try," Orgoch muttered.

Orddu sighed patiently. "Very well, my goslings. We've made our suggestions and we're willing to listen to yours. But mind you, if it's to be a fair exchange, it must be something you prize as much as the Crochan."

"I prize my sword," Taran said. "It is a gift from Dallben and the first blade that is truly mine. For the Crochan I would gladly part with it." He began quickly to unbuckle his belt, but Orddu waved an uninterested hand.

"A sword?" she answered, shaking her head. "Goodness, no, my duck. We already have so many—too many, in fact. And some of them famous weapons of mighty warriors."

"Then," said Taran, with hesitation, "I offer you Lluagor. She is a noble animal." He paused, seeing Orddu's frown. "Or," he added reluctantly in a low voice, "there is my horse, Melynlas, a colt of Melyngar, Prince Gwydion's own steed. None is faster or more surefooted. I treasure Melynlas beyond all others."

"Horses?" said Orddu. "No, that won't do at all. Such a bother feeding them and caring for them. Besides, with Orgoch it's difficult to keep pets about."

Taran was silent for a moment. His face paled as he thought of Adaon's brooch and his hand went protectively to it. "All that remains to me," he began slowly.

"No, no!" Gurgi cried, thrusting his way toward the enchantress and brandishing his wallet. "Take Gurgi's own great treasure! Take bag of crunchings and munchings!"

"Not food," said Orddu. "That won't do either. The only one of us who has the slightest interest in food is Orgoch. And I'm sure your wallet holds nothing to tempt her."

Gurgi looked at Orddu in dismay. "But it is all poor Gurgi has to give." He held out the wallet once again.

The enchantress smiled and shook her head. Gurgi's hands fell to his sides; his shoulders drooped; and he turned mournfully away.

"You must like jewelry," Eilonwy put in quickly. She pulled the ring from her finger and offered it to Orddu. "This is a lovely thing," Eilonwy said. "Prince Gwydion gave it to me. Do you see the stone? It was carved by the Fair Folk."

Orddu took the ring, held it close to her eye, and squinted. "Lovely, lovely," she said. "So pretty. Almost as pretty as you, my lamb. But so much older. No, I'm afraid not. We have a number of them, too. We really don't want any more. Keep it, my chick. One day you may find some use for it, but we surely won't." She gave back the ring to Eilonwy, who sadly replaced it on her finger.

"I do have something else I treasure," Eilonwy went on. She reached into the folds of her cloak and brought out the golden sphere. "Here," she said, turning it in her hands so that it shone with a bright glow. "It's much better than just a light," Eilonwy said. "You see things differently in it, clearer, somehow. It's very useful."

"How sweet of you to offer it to us," said Orddu. "But there again, it's something we don't really need."

"Ladies, ladies!" cried Fflewddur. "You've overlooked a most excellent bargain." He stepped forward and unslung his harp. "I quite understand that bags of food and all such couldn't possibly interest you. But I ask you to consider this harp. You're alone in this gloomy fen," he went on, "and a little music should be just the thing.

"The harp almost plays of itself," Fflewddur continued. He put the beautifully curved instrument on his shoulder, barely touched the strings, and a long, lovely melody filled the air. "You see?" cried the bard. "Nothing to it!"

"Oh, it is nice!" Orwen murmured wistfully. "And think of the songs we could sing to keep ourselves company."

Orddu peered closely at the harp. "I notice a good many of the strings are badly knotted. Has the weather got into them?"

"No, not exactly the weather," said the bard. "With me, they tend to break frequently. But only when I—only when I color the facts a bit. I'm sure you ladies wouldn't have that kind of trouble."

"I can understand you should prize it," Orddu said. "But, if we want music we can always send for a few birds. No, all things considered, it would be a nuisance, keeping it in tune and so on."

"Are you certain you have nothing else?" Orwen asked hopefully.

"That's all," said the disappointed bard. "Absolutely everything. Unless you want the cloaks off our backs."

"Bless you, no!" said Orddu. "It wouldn't be proper in the least for you ducklings to go without them. You'd perish with the cold— and what good would the Crochan be to you then?

"I'm terribly sorry, my chicks," Orddu went on. "It does indeed seem you have nothing to interest us. Very well, we shall keep the Crochan and you shall be on your way."

CHAPTER FIFTEEN

The Black Crochan

"Farewell, my owlets," Orddu said, turning toward the cottage. "Unfortunate you couldn't strike a bargain with us. But that, too, is the way things are. Flutter home to your nest, and give all our love to little Dallben."

"Wait!" Taran called, and strode after her. Eilonwy, realizing his intent, cried out in protest and caught his arm. Gently, Taran put her aside. Orddu stopped and looked back at him.

"There is—there is one thing more," Taran said in a low voice. He stiffened and took a deep breath. "The brooch I wear, the gift of Adaon Son of Taliesin."

"Brooch?" said Orddu, eyeing him curiously. "A brooch, indeed? Yes, that might be more interesting. Just the thing, perhaps. You should have mentioned it sooner."

Taran lifted his head and his eyes met Orddu's. For that instant it seemed to him they were quite alone. He raised his hand slowly to his throat and felt the power of the brooch working within him. "You have been toying with us, Orddu," he whispered. "You saw that I wore Adaon's clasp from the moment we came here. You knew it for what it was."

"Does that matter?" Orddu replied. "It is still your choice, whether you will bargain with it. Yes, we know the brooch well. Menwy Son of Teirgwaedd, first of the bards, fashioned it long ago."

"You could have slain us," Taran murmured, "and taken the clasp."

Orddu smiled sadly. "Do you not understand, poor chicken? Like knowledge, truth, and love themselves, the clasp must be given willingly or its power is broken. And it is, indeed, filled with power. This, too, you must understand. For Menwy the Bard cast a mighty spell on it and filled it with dreams, wisdom, and vision. With such a clasp, a duckling could win much glory and honor. Who can tell? He might rival all the heroes of Prydain, even Gwydion Prince of Don.

"Think carefully, duckling," Orddu said. "Once given up, it shall not come to you again. Will you exchange it for an evil cauldron you intend only to destroy?"

As he held the brooch, Taran recalled with bitter clarity the joys of sight and scent, of dewdrops on a spiderweb, his rescue of the companions from the rock fall, of Gurgi praising his wisdom, the admiring eyes of Eilonwy, and Adaon who had entrusted the brooch to him. Once more there came to him the pride of strength and knowledge. At his feet, the ugly cauldron seemed to mock him.

Taran nodded, barely able to speak. "Yes," he said heavily. "This shall be my bargain." Slowly he undid the clasp at his throat. As he dropped the bit of iron into Orddu's outstretched hand, it was as though a light flickered and died in his heart, and he nearly cried out with the anguish of it.

"Done, my chicken!" Orddu cried. "The brooch for the Crochan!"

About him the companions stood in silence and dismay. Taran's hands clenched. "The Crochan is ours," he said, looking Orddu full in the face. "Is this not so? It is ours, to do with as we please?"

"Why, of course, dear fledgling," Orddu said. "We never break a bargain. It's yours entirely, no question of it."

"In your stables," Taran said, "I saw hammers and iron bars. Will you grant us the use of them? Or," he added bitterly, "must we pay still another price?"

"Use them by all means," replied Orddu. "We'll count that as part of the bargain, for you are a bold chicken, we must admit."

Taran led the companions to the stable and there he paused. "I understand what you were all trying to do," he said quietly, taking their hands in turn. "Each of you would have given up what you treasured most, for my sake. I'm glad Orddu didn't take your harp, Fflewddur," he added. "I know how unhappy you'd be without your music, even more than I without my brooch. And Gurgi, you should never have to tried to sacrifice your food on my account. And Eilonwy, your ring and your bauble are much too useful and beautiful to exchange for an ugly Crochan.

"All of these things," Taran said, "are doubly precious now. And so are you, the best of true comrades." He seized a heavy hammer that was leaning against the wall. "Come now, friends, we have a task to finish."

Armed with iron bars and sledges, the companions hurried back to the cottage and, while the enchantresses looked on curiously, Taran raised his hammer. With all his strength he brought it down on the Crochan.

The hammer rebounded. The cauldron rang like a deep bell of doom, but remained undented. With a cry of anger, Taran struck again. The bard and Eilonwy added a fury of blows, while Gurgi belabored the cauldron with an iron bar.

Despite their efforts, the cauldron showed not the slightest damage. Drenched and exhausted, Taran leaned on his hammer and wiped his streaming face.

"You should have told us, my goslings, what you intended," Orddu called. "You can't do that to the Crochan, you know."

"The cauldron belongs to us," retorted Eilonwy. "Taran has paid more than enough. It's our business if we want to smash it!"

"Naturally," replied Orddu, "and you're quite welcome to hammer and kick it from now until the birds start nesting again. But, my silly goslings, you'll never destroy the Crochan that way. Goodness no, you're going at it all wrong!"

Gurgi, about to crawl inside the Crochan and attack it from within, stopped to listen while Orddu continued.

"Since the Crochan is yours," she said, "you're entitled to know how to dispose of it. There's only one way, though very simple and neat it is."

"Then tell us!" Taran cried. "So that we may put an end to the evil thing!"

"A living person must climb into it," Orddu said. "When he does, the Crochan will shatter. But," she added, "there's only one disagreeable thing about that, the poor duckling who climbs in will never climb out again alive."

With a yelp of terror, Gurgi sprang from the cauldron and scuttled to a safe distance, where he furiously brandished his iron bar and shook his fist at the Crochan.

"Yes," said Orddu with a smile, "that's the way of it. The Crochan only cost you a brooch, but it will cost a life to destroy it. Not only that, but whoever gives up his life to the Crochan must give it willingly, knowing full well what he does.

"And now, my chickens," she went on, "we must really say

farewell. Orgoch is dreadfully sleepy. You had us up so early, you know. Farewell, farewell." She waved a hand and, with the other enchantresses, turned to enter the cottage.

"Stop!" Taran shouted. "Tell us, is there no other way?" He ran to the doorway.

Orddu's head popped out for an instant. "None whatever, my chicken," she said, and for the first time there was a hint of pity in her voice.

The door snapped shut in Taran's face. He pounded in vain; no further reply came from the enchantresses, and even the window suddenly darkened with an impenetrable black fog.

"When Orddu and her friends say farewell," remarked the bard, "they mean it. I doubt we shall see them again." He brightened. "And that's the most cheerful piece of news I've had this morning."

Taran wearily dropped his hammer to the ground. "Surely there must be something else we can do. Though we cannot destroy the Crochan, we dare not part with it."

"Hide it," suggested Fflewddur. "Bury it. And I should say, as soon as possible. You can be quite certain we won't find anyone eager to jump into the thing and break it for us."

Taran shook his head. "No, we cannot hide it. Sooner or later Arawn would find it, and all our efforts would have been useless. Dallben will know," he went on. "He alone has the wisdom to deal with the cauldron. Gwydion himself planned to bring the Crochan to Caer Dallben. Now that must be our task."

Fflewddur nodded. "I suppose that's the only safe thing. But it's a cumbersome beast. I don't see the four of us lugging it along some of those mountain trails."

In front of the silent cottage, the companions led out Lluagor and Melynlas and lashed the cauldron between the two steeds.

Gurgi and Eilonwy guided the heavily laden horses, while Taran and the bard walked, one in front, one behind, to steady the Crochan.

Though eager to be gone from Orddu's cottage, Taran did not dare venture across the Marshes of Morva again. Instead, he determined the companions would travel some distance from the edges of the swamp, keeping to solid ground and following a path half-circling the bog until they reached the moors.

"It's longer," Taran said, "but the Marshes are too treacherous. Last time, Adaon's brooch guided me. Now," he added with a sigh, "I'm afraid I'd lead us to the same fate as the Huntsmen."

"That's rather a good idea!" cried the bard. "Not for us," he added quickly, "for the Crochan. Sink the beastly pot in the quicksand!"

"No thank you!" answered Eilonwy. "By the time we found quicksand, we'd be sinking along with the Crochan. If you're tired, we can change off and you lead Melynlas."

"Not at all, not at all," grunted Fflewddur. "It's not as heavy as all that. In fact, I find the exercise bracing, quite invigorating. A Fflam never flags!"

At this, a harp string broke, but the bard gave it no heed, busy as he was in holding his side of the swaying cauldron.

Taran trudged in silence, speaking only to call directions to Eilonwy and Gurgi. They continued with few moments of rest throughout the day. Nevertheless by sunset Taran realized they had covered only a little distance and had barely reached the broad moorlands. He was aware, too, of his own fatigue, heavy as the Crochan itself, a weariness he had never noticed while he had worn Adaon's brooch.

They camped on an open heath, cold and barren, shrouded with mist drifting from the Marshes of Morva. There they unroped the Crochan from the tired horses and Gurgi brought out food from the wallet. After the meal, Fflewddur's spirits revived. Although shivering in the chill and dampness, the bard put his harp to his shoulder and attempted to cheer the companions with a merry song.

Taran, usually eager to listen to the bard's music, sat apart, gloomily watching the cauldron. After a time Eilonwy drew near and put her hand on his shoulder.

"I realize it's no consolation to you," she said, "but if you look at it in one way, you didn't give up a thing to the enchantresses, not really. You did exchange the clasp and everything that went along with it. But, don't you see, all those things came from the clasp itself; they weren't inside of you.

"I think," she added, "it would have been much worse giving up a summer day. That's part of you, I mean. I know I shouldn't want to give up a single one of mine. Or even a winter day, for the matter of that. So, when you come right down to it, Orddu didn't take anything from *you*; why, you're still yourself and you can't deny that!"

"Yes," Taran answered. "I am still only an Assistant Pig-Keeper. I should have known that anything else was too good to last."

"That may be true," said Eilonwy, "but as far as being an Assistant Pig-Keeper is concerned, I think you're a perfectly marvelous one. Believe me, there's no question in my mind you're the best Assistant Pig-Keeper in all Prydain. How many others there are, I'm sure I don't know, but that's beside the point. And I doubt a single one of them would have done what you did."

"I could not have done otherwise," Taran said, "not if we were to gain the cauldron. Orddu said they were interested in things as they are," he went on. "I believe now they are concerned with things as they must be.

"Adaon knew there was a destiny laid on him," Taran continued, turning to Eilonwy, his voice growing firmer, "and he did not turn from it, though it cost him his life.

"Very well," he declared. "If there is a destiny laid on me, I shall face it. I hope only that I may face it as well as Adaon did his."

"But don't forget," added Eilonwy, "no matter what else happens, you won the cauldron for Gwydion and Dallben and all of us. That's one thing nobody can take away from you. Why, for that alone you have every reason to be proud."

Taran nodded. "Yes, this much have I done." He said no more and Eilonwy quietly left him there.

For long after the others had gone to sleep, Taran sat staring at the Crochan. He thought carefully over all Eilonwy had told him; his despair lightened a little and pride stirred within him. Soon the cauldron would be in Gwydion's hands and the long task ended. "This much have I done," Taran repeated to himself, and new strength budded in his heart.

Nevertheless, as the wind moaned across the heath and the Crochan loomed before him like an iron shadow, he thought once again of the brooch, and he buried his face in his hands and wept.

CHAPTER SIXTEEN

The River

This night's sleep refreshed Taran but little and hardly blunted the edge of his weariness. Nevertheless, at dawn he roused the companions and with much effort they began roping the Crochan to Lluagor and Melynlas. When they finished, Taran glanced around him uneasily.

"There is no concealment for us on these moors," he said. "I had hoped we might keep to the flatlands where our journey would be easier. But I fear that Arawn will have his gwythaints seeking the Crochan. Sooner or later they will find us, and here they could fall on us like hawks on chickens."

"Please don't mention chickens," said the bard with a sour grimace. "I had quite enough of that from Orddu."

"Gurgi will protect kind master!" shouted Gurgi.

Taran smiled and put a hand on Gurgi's shoulder. "I know you'll do your best," he said. "But all of us together are no match for even one gwythaint." Taran shook his head. "No," he said reluctantly, "I think we had better turn north to the Forest of Idris. It's the longest way around, but at least it would give us some cover."

Eilonwy agreed. "It's not usually wise to go in the direction opposite to where you want to be," she said. "But you can be sure I'd rather not fight gwythaints."

"Lead on, then," said Fflewddur. "A Fflam never falters! Though what my aching bones might do is another matter!"

Crossing the moorlands, the companions journeyed without difficulties, but once within the Forest of Idris the Crochan grew more burdensome. Although the trees and bushes offered concealment and protection, the paths were narrow. Lluagor and Melynlas stumbled often and, despite their most valiant efforts, they could barely drag the cauldron through the brush.

Taran called a halt. "Our horses have borne all they can," he said, patting the lathered neck of Melynlas. "Now it is our turn to help them. I wish Doli were here." He sighed. "I'm sure he'd find an easier way of carrying the Crochan. He'd think of something clever. Like making a sling out of branches and vines."

"There!" cried Eilonwy. "You've just said it yourself! You're doing amazingly well without Adaon's brooch!"

With their swords Taran and the bard cut stout branches, while Eilonwy and Gurgi stripped vines from the tree trunks. Taran's spirits lifted when he saw the sling take shape according to his plan. The companions hoisted up the Crochan and set off again. But even with the sling, and all their strength, their progress was slow and painful.

"Oh, poor weary arms!" moaned Gurgi. "Oh, moilings and toilings! This evil pot is a cruel and wicked master to us all! Oh, sorrow! Fainting Gurgi will never leave Caer Dallben again unbidden!"

Taran gritted his teeth, as the rough branches bit into his shoulders. To him, too, it seemed as if the ugly, heavy cauldron had gained some strange life of its own. The Crochan, squat and blood-darkened, lurched behind him as he stumbled through the brush. It caught on jutting tree limbs, as though eagerly clutching them to itself. Often, at these sudden checks, the companions lost their footing and went sprawling. Then, laboriously, they were obliged to set the Crochan back in its sling once again. Though the weather was chill enough to turn their breath white, their clothing was drenched with sweat and nearly ripped to shreds by the grasping brambles.

The trees had begun to grow more dense, and the ground rose toward the comb of a hill. For Taran, the Crochan seemed to gain weight with every pace. Its leering, gaping mouth taunted him, and the cauldron dragged at his strength as he heaved and struggled along the ascending trail.

The companions had nearly reached the crest of the hill when one of the carrier branches snapped. The Crochan plunged to the ground and Taran fell headlong. Painfully picking himself up and rubbing his shoulder, he stared at the spiteful cauldron and shook his head.

"No use," Taran gasped. "We'll never get it through the forest. No sense trying."

"You sound like Gwystyl," Eilonwy remarked. "If I didn't have my eyes open, I could barely tell the difference."

"Gwystyl!" cried the bard, looking ruefully at his blistered hands. "I envy that fellow in his rabbit warren! Sometimes I think he had quite the right idea."

"We are too few to carry such a burden," Taran said hopelessly. "With another horse or another pair of hands there might be a chance. We are only deceiving ourselves if we think we can bring the Crochan to Caer Dallben."

"That may be true," Eilonwy sighed wearily. "But I don't know what else we can do, except keep on deceiving ourselves. And perhaps by that time we'll be home."

Taran cut a new branch for the sling, but his heart was as heavy as the Crochan itself. And, as the companions wrestled their burden over the hill and descended into a deep valley, Taran nearly sank to the ground in despair. Before them, like a brown, menacing serpent, stretched a turbulent river.

Taran stared grimly at the choppy waters for a moment, then turned away. "There is a destiny laid on us that the Crochan shall never reach Caer Dallben."

"Nonsense!" cried Eilonwy. "If you stop now, then you've given up Adaon's brooch for nothing! That's worse than putting a necklace on an owl and letting it fly away!"

"If I'm not mistaken," said Fflewddur helpfully, "that must be the River Tevvyn. I've crossed it farther to the north, where it takes its source. Surprising, the bits of information you pick up as a wandering bard."

"Alas, it does us no good, my friend," Taran said, "unless we could turn north again and cross where the river is less wide."

"Afraid that wouldn't answer," said Fflewddur. "We'd have the mountains to go over, that way. If we're to cross at all, we shall have to do it here."

"It seems a little shallower down that way," said Eilonwy, pointing to a spot where the river curved around a sedge-covered bank. "Very well, Taran of Caer Dallben," she said, "what shall it be? We can't just sit here until gwythaints, or something even more disagreeable, find us, and we certainly can't go back to Orddu and offer to exchange the Crochan again."

Taran took a deep breath. "If you are all willing," he said, "we shall try to cross."

✥

Slowly, struggling under the cruel weight, the companions brought the Crochan to the riverbank. While Gurgi, leading the horses, cautiously set one foot, then the other, into the stream, Taran and the bard shouldered the sling. Eilonwy followed beside them to steady the swaying cauldron. The icy water slashed at Taran's legs like a knife. He dug his heels into the riverbed, seeking a firmer foothold. He plunged deeper; behind him, the straining, grunting Fflewddur did his best to avoid dropping his end of the sling. The chill of the river took Taran's breath away. His head spun, the branches nearly slipped from his numb fingers.

For one moment of terror he felt himself falling. His foot found a rock and he braced himself on it. The vines creaked and tensed as the weight of the cauldron shifted. The companions were in mid-stream now and the water rose only to their waists. Taran raised his streaming face. The opposite bank was not far; the ground appeared smoother, the forest not as dense.

"Soon there!" he cried, taking heart anew. Gurgi, he saw, had already led the horses from the water and was turning back to help the toiling companions.

Closer to the bank the river bottom turned stony. Blindly, Taran picked his way through the treacherous rocks. Ahead rose a number of high boulders and he warily guided the Crochan past them. Gurgi was reaching out his hands when Taran heard a sharp cry from the bard. The cauldron lurched. With all his strength Taran heaved forward. Eilonwy seized the cauldron by its handle and tugged desperately. Taran flung himself to dry ground.

The Crochan rolled to its side and sank in the muddy shallows.

Taran turned back to help Fflewddur. The bard, who had fallen heavily against the boulders, was struggling to shore. His face was white with pain; his right arm hung uselessly at his side.

"Is it broken? Is it broken?" Fflewddur moaned as Taran and Eilonwy hurried to lead him up the bank.

"I'll be able to tell in a moment," Taran said, helping the stumbling bard to sit down and prop his back against an alder. He opened Fflewddur's cloak, slit the sleeve of his jacket, and carefully examined the damaged arm. Taran saw quickly that the bard's fall had not only been severe but that one of the cauldron's legs had given him a deep gash in his side. "Yes," Taran said gravely, "I'm afraid it is."

At this the bard set up a loud lament and bowed his head. "Terrible, terrible," he groaned. "A Fflam is always cheerful, but this is too much to bear."

"It was a bad accident," Eilonwy said, trying to hide her concern, "but you mustn't take on so. It can be fixed. We'll bind it up."

"Useless!" cried Fflewddur in despair. "It will never be the same! Oh, it is the fault of that beastly Crochan! The wretched thing struck at me deliberately, I'm sure!"

"You'll be all right, I promise you," Taran reassured the sorrowful bard. He tore several wide strips from his cloak. "Good as new in a little while," he added. "Of course, you won't be able to move your arm until it's healed."

"Arm?" cried Fflewddur. "It's not my *arm* that worries me! It's my *harp!*"

"Your harp is in a better state than you are," said Eilonwy, taking the bard's instrument from his shoulder and putting it in his lap.

"Great Belin, but you gave me a shock!" Fflewddur said, caressing the harp with his free hand. "Arms? Naturally, they heal themselves with no trouble at all. I've had a dozen broken—yes, well, that is to say I snapped my wrist once during a little swordplay—in any case, I have two arms. But only one harp!" The bard heaved an immense sigh of relief. "Indeed, I feel better already."

Despite Fflewddur's brave grin, Taran saw the bard was suffering more than he chose to admit. Quickly and gently Taran finished making a splint and winding the strips about it, then brought herbs from Lluagor's saddlebag. "Chew these," he told Fflewddur. "They will ease your pain. And you'd better stay perfectly still for a while."

"Lie still?" cried the bard. "Not now, of all times! We must fish that vile pot out of the river!"

Taran shook his head. "The three of us will try to raise it. With a broken arm even a Fflam wouldn't be much help."

"By no means!" cried Fflewddur. "A Fflam is always helpful!" He struggled to raise himself from the ground, winced, and fell back again. Gasping with the pain of his exertion, he looked dolefully at his injury.

Taran uncoiled the ropes and, with Gurgi and Eilonwy following, made his way to the shallows. The Crochan lay half submerged in the water. The current eddied around its gaping mouth and the cauldron seemed to be muttering defiance. The sling, Taran saw, was undamaged, but the cauldron was caught firmly between the boulders. He looped a rope and cast it over a jutting leg, directing Gurgi and Eilonwy to pull when he signaled.

He waded into the river, bent, and tried to thrust his shoulder under the cauldron. Gurgi and Eilonwy hauled with all their strength. The Crochan did not move.

Soaked to the skin, his hands numb, Taran wrestled vainly with the cauldron. Breathless, he staggered back to shore where he attached ropes to Lluagor and Melynlas.

Once again Taran returned to the icy stream. He shouted to Eilonwy, who led the horses away from the river. The ropes tightened; the steeds labored; Taran heaved and tugged at the immovable cauldron. The bard had managed to regain his feet and lent what effort he could. Gurgi and Eilonwy took their places in the water beside Taran, but the Crochan resisted the force of all their muscles.

In despair Taran signaled for them to stop. Heavy-hearted, the companions returned to shore.

"We shall camp here for the rest of the day," Taran said. "Tomorrow, when we have our strength back, we can try again. There may be some other way of getting it out, I don't know. It is tightly wedged and everything we do seems to make it worse."

He looked toward the river, where the cauldron crouched like a glowering beast of prey.

"It is a thing of evil," Taran said, "and has brought nothing but evil. Now, at the last, I fear it has defeated us."

He turned away. Behind him the bushes rustled. Taran spun around, his hand on his sword.

A figure stepped from the edge of the forest.

CHAPTER SEVENTEEN

The Choice

It was Ellidyr. With Islimach following, he strode to the river-bank. Dry mud caked his tawny hair and grimed his face. His cheeks and hands had been cruelly slashed; his bloodstained jacket was half ripped from his shoulders, and he wore no cloak. Dark-ringed, his eyes glittered feverishly. Ellidyr halted before the speechless companions, threw back his head, and glanced scorn-fully at them.

"Well met," he said in a hoarse voice, "brave company of scare-crows." His lips drew back in a taut, bitter grin. "The pig-boy, the scullery maid—I do not see the dreamer."

"What do you here?" Taran cried, facing him angrily. "You dare speak of Adaon? He is slain and lies beneath his burial mound. You have betrayed us, Son of Pen-Llarcau! Where were you when the Huntsmen set upon us? When another sword would have turned the balance? The price was Adaon's life, a better man than you shall ever be!"

Ellidyr did not reply, but moved stiffly past Taran and squatted down near the pile of saddlebags. "Give me food," he said sharply. "Roots and rain water have been my meat and drink."

"Evil traitor!" shouted Gurgi, leaping to his feet. "There are no crunchings and munchings for wicked villain, no, no!"

"Hold your tongue," said Ellidyr, "or you shall hold your head."

"Give him food, as he asks," Taran ordered.

Muttering furiously, Gurgi obeyed and opened the wallet.

"And just because we're feeding you," cried Eilonwy, "don't think you're welcome to it!"

"The scullery maid is not pleased to see me," said Ellidyr. "She shows temper."

"Can't say I really blame her," rejoined Fflewddur. "And I don't see that you should expect anything else. You've done us a bad turn. Would you have us hold a festival?"

"The harp-scraper is still with you, at least," Ellidyr said, seizing the food from Gurgi. "But I see he is a bird with a wing down."

"Birds again," murmured the bard with a shudder. "Shall I never be allowed to forget Orddu?"

"Why do you seek us?" Taran demanded. "You were content to leave us once. What brings you here now?"

"Seek you?" Ellidyr laughed harshly. "I seek the Marshes of Morva."

"Well, you're a long way from them," Eilonwy cried. "But if you're in a hurry to get there—as I hope you are—I'll be glad to give you directions. And while you're there, I suggest you find Orddu, Orwen, and Orgoch. They'll be happier to see you than we are."

Ellidyr wolfed down his food and settled himself against the saddlebags. "That is better," he said. "Now there is a bit more life in me."

"Enough to take you wherever you happen to be going," snapped Eilonwy.

"And wherever you happen to be going," replied Ellidyr, "I wish you the joy of your journey. You shall find Huntsmen enough to satisfy you."

"What," cried Taran, "are the Huntsmen still abroad?"

"Yes, pig-boy," Ellidyr answered. "All Annuvin is astir. The Huntsmen I have outrun, a noble game of hare and hounds. The gwythaints have had their sport of me," he added with a contemptuous laugh, "though it cost them two of their number. But enough remain to offer you good hunting, if that is your pleasure."

"I hope you didn't lead them to us," Eilonwy began.

"I led them nowhere," said Ellidyr, "least of all to you, since I did not know you were here. When the gwythaints and I parted company, I assure you I gave little heed to the path I chose."

"You can still choose your path," said Eilonwy, "so long as it leads you from us. And I hope you follow it as swiftly as you did when you sneaked away."

"Sneaked away?" laughed Ellidyr. "A Son of Pen-Llarcau does not sneak. You were too slow-footed for me. There were matters of urgency to attend to."

"Your own glory!" Taran replied sharply. "You thought of nothing else. At least, Ellidyr, speak the truth."

"It is true enough I meant to go to the Marshes of Morva," Ellidyr said with a bitter smile. "And true enough I did not find them. Though I should, had the Huntsmen not barred my way.

"From the scullery maid's words," Ellidyr went on, "I gather you have been to Morva."

Taran nodded. "Yes, we have been there. Now we return to Caer Dallben."

Ellidyr laughed again. "And you, too, have failed. But, since your journey was the longer, I ask you which of us wasted more of his labor and pains?"

"Failed?" cried Taran. "We did not fail! The cauldron is ours! There it lies," he added, pointing past the riverbank to the black hump of the Crochan.

Ellidyr sprang to his feet and looked across the water. "How, then!" he shouted wrathfully. "Have you cheated me once more?" His face darkened with rage. "Do I risk my life again so that a pig-boy may rob me of my prize?" His eyes were frenzied and he made to seize Taran by the throat.

Taran struck away his hand. "I have never cheated you, Son of Pen-Llarcau!" he cried. "*Your* prize? Risk *your* life? We have lost life and shed blood for the cauldron. Yes, a heavy price has been paid, heavier than you know, Prince of Pen-Llarcau."

Ellidyr seemed to strangle on his rage. He stood without moving, his face working and twitching. But he soon forced himself to seem again cold and haughty, though his hands still trembled.

"So, pig-boy," he said in a low, rasping voice, "you have found the cauldron after all. Yet, indeed, it would seem to belong more to the river than to you. Who but a pig-boy would leave it stranded thus? Did you not have wits enough or strength enough to smash it, that you must bear it with you?"

"The Crochan cannot be destroyed unless a man give up his life in it," Taran answered. "We have wits enough to know it must be put safely in Dallben's hands."

"Would you be a hero, pig-boy?" asked Ellidyr. "Why do you not climb into it yourself? Surely you are bold enough. Or are you a coward at heart, when the test is put upon you?"

Taran disregarded Ellidyr's taunt. "We need your help," he said urgently. "Our strength fails us. Help us bring the Crochan to Caer Dallben. Or at least aid us to move it to the riverbank."

"Help you?" Ellidyr threw back his head and laughed wildly.

"Help you? So that a pig-boy may strut before Gwydion and boast of his deeds? And a Prince of Pen-Llarcau play the churl? No, you shall have no help from me! I warned you to take your own part! Do it now, pig-boy!"

Eilonwy screamed and pointed to the sky. "Gwythaints!"

A flight of three gwythaints soared high above the trees. Racing with the wind-driven clouds, the gigantic birds sped closer. Taran and Eilonwy caught up Fflewddur between them and stumbled into the bushes. Gurgi, almost witless with fear, pulled on the horses' bridles, leading them to the safety of the trees. While Ellidyr followed, the gwythaints swooped downward, the wind rattling in their flashing feathers.

With harsh and fearsome shrieking, the gwythaints circled around the cauldron, blotting out the sun with their black wings. One of the ferocious birds came to rest on the Crochan and for an instant remained poised there, beating its wings. The gwythaints made no attempt to attack the companions, but circled once again, then drove skyward. They veered north and the mountains quickly hid them.

Pale and shaking, Taran stepped from the bushes. "They have found what they were seeking," he said. "Arawn will soon know the Crochan waits to be plucked from our hands." He turned to Ellidyr. "Help us," he asked again, "I beg you. We dare not lose a moment."

Ellidyr shrugged and strode down the riverbank into the shallows where he looked closely at the half-sunken Crochan. "It can be moved," he said when he returned. "But not by you, pig-boy. You will need the strength of Islimach added to your own steeds— and you will need mine."

"Lend us your strength, then," Taran pleaded. "Let us raise the

Crochan and be gone from here before more of Arawn's servants reach it."

"Perhaps I shall; perhaps I shall not," answered Ellidyr with a strange look in his eyes. "Did you pay a price to gain the cauldron? Very well, you shall pay another one.

"Hear me, pig-boy," he went on. "If I help you bear the cauldron to Caer Dallben, it shall be on my own conditions."

"This is no time for conditions," cried Eilonwy. "We don't want to listen to your conditions, Ellidyr. We'll find our own way to get the Crochan out. Or we'll stay here with it and one of us can go back and bring Gwydion."

"Stay here and be slain," Ellidyr replied. "No, it must be done now, and done as I say or not at all."

He turned to Taran. "These are my conditions," he said. "The Crochan is mine, and you shall be under my command. It is I who found it, not you, pig-boy. It is I who fought for it and won it. So you shall say to Gwydion and the others. And you shall all swear the most binding oath."

"No, we shall not!" cried Eilonwy. "You ask us to lie so that you may steal the Crochan and steal our own efforts with it! You are mad, Ellidyr!"

"Not mad, scullery maid," said Ellidyr, his eyes blazing, "but weary to my death. Do you hear me? All my life have I been forced into the second rank. I have been put aside, slighted. Honor? It has been denied me at every turn. But this time I shall not let the prize slip from my fingers."

"Adaon saw a black beast on your shoulders," Taran said quietly. "And I, too, have seen it. I see it now, Ellidyr."

"I care nothing for your black beast!" shouted Ellidyr. "I care for my honor."

"Do you think," Taran said, "I care nothing for mine?"

"What is the honor of a pig-boy?" laughed Ellidyr, "compared to the honor of a prince?"

"I have paid for my honor," answered Taran, his voice rising, "more dearly than you would pay for yours. Do you ask me now to cast it away?"

"You, pig-boy, dared reproach me for seeking glory," said Ellidyr. "Yet you yourself cling to it with your dirty hands. I shall not tarry here. My terms or nothing. Make your choice."

Taran stood silent. Eilonwy seized Ellidyr by the jacket. "How dare you ask such a price?"

Ellidyr drew away. "Let the pig-boy decide. It is up to him whether he will pay it."

"If I swear this," Taran said, turning to the companions, "you must swear along with me. Once given, I will not break an oath, and it would be even more to my shame if I broke this one. Before I can decide, I must know whether you, too, will bind yourselves. On this we must all agree."

No one spoke. At length, Fflewddur murmured, "I put the decision in your hands and abide by what you do."

Gurgi nodded his head solemnly.

"I shall not lie!" Eilonwy cried, "not for this traitor and deserter."

"It is not for him," Taran said quietly, "but for the sake of our quest."

"It isn't right," Eilonwy began, tears starting in her eyes.

"We do not speak of rightness," Taran answered. "We speak of a task to be finished."

Eilonwy looked away. "Fflewddur has said the choice is yours," she murmured at last. "I must say the same."

For a long moment Taran did not speak. All the anguish he had felt when Adaon's brooch had left his hands returned to him. And he recalled Eilonwy's words in his blackest despair, the girl's voice telling him that nothing could take away what he had done. Yet this was the very price Ellidyr demanded.

Taran bowed his head. "The cauldron, Ellidyr, is yours," he said slowly. "We are at your command, and all things shall be as you say. Thus we swear."

Heavy-hearted and silent, the companions followed Ellidyr's orders and once again lashed ropes around the sunken Crochan. Ellidyr hitched the three horses side by side, then attached the lines to them. While Fflewddur held the bridles with his uninjured hand, the companions waded into the shallows.

Ellidyr, standing up to his knees in the rushing water, commanded Taran, Eilonwy, and Gurgi to post themselves on either side of the Crochan and keep it from slipping back against the boulders. He signaled an order to the waiting bard, then bent to his own task.

As he had done with Melynlas long before, Ellidyr thrust his shoulders as far below the cauldron as the rocks allowed. His body tensed; the veins rose to bursting on his streaming forehead. Still the cauldron did not yield. Beside him, Taran and Eilonwy heaved vainly at the sling.

Gasping for breath, Ellidyr turned once more to the Crochan. The sling creaked against the boulders; the ropes strained. Ellidyr's shoulders were cut and bleeding, his face deathly white. He choked out another command to the companions; his muscles trembled in a final effort.

With a cry, he pitched forward into the water, stumbling to gain his balance. Then he gave an exultant shout. The cauldron had lifted free.

Desperately the companions labored to bring the Crochan to shore. Ellidyr seized one end of the sling and thrust ahead. The cauldron skidded to dry, firm ground.

On the riverbank they quickly roped the sling between Melynlas and Lluagor. Ellidyr hitched up Islimach as the leading horse, to guide the others and bear a share of the weight.

Until then Ellidyr's eyes had burned with triumph, but now his face changed.

"My cauldron has been won back from the river," he said, with a curious glance at Taran. "But I think perhaps I was too hasty. You met my terms too quickly," he added. "Tell me, what is in your mind, pig-boy?" Rage filled him again. "I know well enough! Once more you would try to cheat me!"

"You have my oath," Taran began.

"What is the oath of a pig-boy?" Ellidyr said. "You gave it; you will break it!"

"Speak for yourself," Eilonwy said angrily. "That's what you would do, Prince of Pen-Llarcau. But we are not like you."

"The cauldron needed all of us to raise it," Ellidyr continued, lowering his voice. "But does it now need all of us to carry it? A few would serve," he added. "Yes, yes—only a few. Perhaps only one, if he were strong enough.

"Was my price too low?" he went on, spinning around to face Taran.

"Ellidyr," Taran cried, "you are truly mad."

"Yes!" laughed Ellidyr. "Mad to believe your word alone! The price must be silence, utter silence!" His hand moved to his sword.

"Yes, pig-boy, I knew in time we should have to face one another."

He lunged forward, his sword out and raised. Before Taran could draw his own blade, Ellidyr swung viciously and pressed to the attack. Taran stumbled down the riverbank and leaped to a boulder, feverishly grasping for his weapon. Ellidyr strode into the water while the companions raced to stop him.

As Ellidyr swung his blade again, Taran lost his footing and toppled from the boulder. He tried to rise, but the stones slipped from under him and he stumbled backward. He threw up his hands. The current was clutching at him and he fell. The sharp edge of a rock loomed up, and he knew no more.

CHAPTER EIGHTEEN

The Loss

It was night when Taran came to his senses. He found himself propped against a log, a cloak wrapped around him. His head throbbed; his body ached. Eilonwy was bending over him anxiously. Taran blinked his eyes and tried to sit up. For some moments his memory held only a mingling of sights and sounds, of rushing water, a stone, a shout; his head still whirled. A yellow light shone in his eyes. He realized, as his mind gradually cleared, that the girl had lit the golden sphere and had set it on the log. Beside him, a small fire blazed. Crouched next to it, the bard and Gurgi fed twigs to the flames.

"I'm glad you decided to wake up," Eilonwy said, trying to appear cheerful, as Fflewddur and Gurgi came to kneel beside Taran. "You swallowed so much of the river we were afraid we'd never be able to pump it out of you, and that rap on your head didn't help matters."

"The Crochan!" Taran gasped. "Ellidyr!" He looked around him. "This fire," he murmured, "we dare not show a light—Arawn's warriors . . ."

"It was either build a fire or let you freeze to death," said the bard, "so of course we decided on the first. At this point," he added with a wry grin, "I doubt it can make too much difference. Since the cauldron is out of our hands, I don't believe Arawn will have quite the same interest in us. Happily, I might say."

"Where is the Crochan?" Taran asked. Despite his spinning head, he raised himself from the log.

"It is with Ellidyr," said Eilonwy.

"And if you ask where *he* is," put in the bard, "we can answer you very quickly: we do not know."

"Wicked prince goes off with wicked pot," Gurgi added. "Yes, yes, with ridings and stridings!"

"Good riddance to them," agreed Fflewddur. "I don't know which is worse, the Crochan or Ellidyr. Now, at least, they're both together."

"You let him go?" Taran cried in alarm. He put his hands to his head. "You let him steal the Crochan?"

"*Let* is hardly the word, my friend," the bard answered ruefully.

"You seem to have forgotten," Eilonwy added. "Ellidyr was trying to kill you. It's a good thing you fell into the river, because I can tell you the goings-on weren't very pleasant on the shore.

"It was terrible, as a matter of fact," the girl went on. "We'd all started after Ellidyr—by that time you were already floating down the river like a twig in a—well, like a twig in a river. We tried to save you, but Ellidyr turned on us.

"I'm certain he meant to kill us," Eilonwy said. "You should have seen his face, and his eyes. He was furious. Worse than that. Fflewddur tried to stand against him . . ."

"That villain has the strength of ten!" said the bard. "I could barely draw my sword—it's clumsy when you have a broken arm, you understand. But I faced him! A dreadful clash of weapons! You've never seen the prowess of an outraged Fflam! Another moment and I should have had him at my mercy—in a manner of speaking," the bard added quickly. "He knocked me sprawling."

"And Gurgi fought, too! Yes, yes, with smitings and bitings!"

"Poor Gurgi," said Eilonwy, "he did his best. But Ellidyr picked him up and tossed him against a tree. When I tried to draw my bow, he snatched it away and snapped it in his hands."

"He chased us into the woods, after that," Fflewddur said. "I've never seen a man in such a frenzy. Shouting at the top of his voice, calling us robbers and oath-breakers, and that we were trying to keep him in second place, that's all he's able to say or think now, if you choose to call that thinking."

Taran shook his head sadly. "I fear the black beast has swallowed him up as Adaon warned," he said. "I pity Ellidyr from the bottom of my heart."

"I should pity him more," muttered Fflewddur, "if he hadn't tried to slice off my head."

"For long, I hated him," Taran said, "but in the little while I bore Adaon's brooch, I believe I saw him more clearly. His heart is unhappy and tormented. Nor shall I forget what he said to me: that I taunted him for seeking glory yet clung to it myself." Taran spread his hands in front of him. "With dirty hands," he said heavily.

"Pay no heed to what Ellidyr says," Eilonwy cried. "After what he made us do, he has no right to blame anyone for anything."

"And yet," Taran said softly, almost to himself, "he spoke the truth."

"Did he?" said Eilonwy. "It was only too true, for his own honor he would have slain us all."

"We managed to escape from him," Fflewddur continued. "That is, he finally stopped pursuing us. When we came back, the horses,

the Crochan, and Ellidyr were gone. After that we followed down
the river looking for you. You hadn't gone far. But I'm still amazed
that anyone can swallow so much water in such a short distance."

"We must find him!" Taran cried. "We dare not let him keep the
Crochan! You should have left me and gone after him." He tried to
climb to his feet. "Come now, there is no time to lose!"

Fflewddur shook his head "I'm afraid there's no use in it, as our
friend Gwystyl might say. There's not a sign of him anywhere. We
have no idea where he planned to go or what he had in mind to do.
He has too long a start on us. And, though I hate to admit it, I
don't believe any one of us, or all of us together, could do very
much against him." The bard glanced at his broken arm. "We're
hardly in the best way to deal with the Crochan or Ellidyr, even if
we found them."

Taran stared silently into the fire. "You, too, speak the truth, my
friend," he said with great gloom. "You have all done more than I
could ever ask. Alas, much better than I. Yes, it would be useless
now to seek Ellidyr, as useless as our quest has been. We have for-
feited all for nothing—Adaon's brooch, our honor, and now the
Crochan itself. We shall return to Caer Dallben empty-handed.
Perhaps Ellidyr was right," he murmured. "It is not fitting for a
pig-boy to seek the same honor as a prince."

"Pig-boy!" Eilonwy cried indignantly. "Don't ever speak of yourself that way, Taran of Caer Dallben. No matter what has happened, you're not a pig-boy; you're an Assistant Pig-Keeper! That's
honor in itself! Not that they don't mean the same thing, when
you come right down to it," she said, "but one is proud and the
other isn't. Since you have a choice, take the proud one!"

Taran said nothing for a time, then raised his head to Eilonwy.

"Adaon once told me there is more honor in a field well plowed than in a field steeped in blood." As he spoke, his heart seemed to lighten. "I see now that what he said was true above all. I do not begrudge Ellidyr his prize. I, too, shall seek honor. But I shall seek it where I know it will be found."

The companions passed the night in the forest and next morning turned southward across gentler land. They saw neither Huntsmen nor gwythaints, and they made little attempt at concealment; for, as the bard had said, the forces of Arawn sought the Crochan and not a pitiful band of stragglers. Unburdened, they moved more easily, though without Lluagor and Melynlas their pace on foot was slow and painful. Taran trudged silently, his head bowed against the bitter wind. Dead leaves drove against his face, but he paid them no heed, filled as he was with the distress of his own thoughts.

Some while after midday Taran caught sight of movement among the trees covering a hill crest. Foreseeing danger, he urged the companions to hurry across the open meadow and find cover in a thicket. But before they could reach it, a party of horsemen appeared at the rise and galloped toward them. Taran and the bard drew their swords, Gurgi nocked an arrow into his bowstring, and the weary band made ready to defend themselves as best they could.

Fflewddur suddenly gave a great shout and waved his sword excitedly. "Put up your weapons!" he cried. "We're safe at last! These are Morgant's warriors! They bear the colors of the House of Madoc!"

The warriors pounded closer. Taran, too, cried out with relief. They were indeed King Morgant's riders, and at their head rode

King Morgant himself. As they reined up beside the companions, Taran hurried to Morgant's steed and dropped to one knee.

"Well met, Sire," he cried. "We feared your men were servants of Arawn."

King Morgant swung down from the saddle. His black cloak was torn and travel-stained, his face haggard and grim, but his eyes still held the fierce pride of a hawk. A trace of a smile flickered on his lips. "But you would have stood against us nonetheless," he said, raising Taran to his feet.

"What of Prince Gwydion, of Coll?" Taran asked quickly and with sudden uneasiness. "We were separated at Dark Gate and have had no word of them. Adaon, alas, is slain. And Doli, too, I fear."

"Of the dwarf, there has been no trace," answered Morgant. "Lord Gwydion and Coll Son of Collfrewr are safe. They seek you even now. Though," Morgant added, with another half smile, "it has been my good fortune to find you.

"The Huntsmen of Annuvin pressed us sharply at Dark Gate," Morgant went on. "At last we fought free of them and began to make our way toward Caer Cadarn, where Lord Gwydion hoped you would join us.

"We had not reached there," said Morgant, "before we had word of you, and that you had taken it on yourselves to go to the Marshes of Morva. That was a bold venture, Taran of Caer Dallben," Morgant added, "as bold, perhaps, as it was ill-advised. You should learn that a warrior owes obedience to his lord."

"It did not seem we could do otherwise," Taran protested. "We had to find the Crochan before Arawn. Would you not have done the same?"

Morgant nodded curtly. "I do not reproach your spirit, but would have you understand that Lord Gwydion himself would hesitate to make a decision of such weight. We would have known nothing of your movements had not Gwystyl of the Fair Folk brought us news. Lord Gwydion and I separated then to search for you."

"Gwystyl?" Eilonwy interrupted. "Not Gwystyl! Why, he wouldn't have done the least thing for us—until Doli threatened to squeeze him! Gwystyl! All he wanted was to be let alone and hide in his wretched burrow!"

Morgant turned to her. "You speak without knowledge, Princess. Among all who hold the way posts, Gwystyl of the Fair Folk is the shrewdest and bravest. Did you believe King Eiddileg would trust a lesser servant so close to Annuvin? But," he added, "if you misjudged him, it was his intention that you do so.

"As for the Crochan itself," Morgant went on, as Taran looked at him in amazement, "though you failed to bring it from Morva, Prince Ellidyr has done us noble service. Yes," Morgant added quickly, "my warriors came upon him near the River Tevvyn in the course of our search. From his words, I understood that you were drowned and your companions scattered, and that he bore the cauldron from Morva."

"That's not true," Eilonwy began, her eyes flashing angrily.

"Be silent!" Taran cried.

"No, I will not be silent," retorted Eilonwy, spinning around to face Taran. "You aren't going to tell me you still think you're bound by that oath you made us all swear!"

"What does she mean?" Morgant asked. His eyes narrowed and he studied Taran closely.

"I'll tell you what I mean!" Eilonwy answered, heedless of Taran's protest. "It's very simple. Taran paid for it, and paid dearly. We carried it almost on our backs every step of the way from Morva, until Ellidyr came along. He helped us—he certainly did that, just the way a robber helps you tidy up your chamber! That's the truth of it, and I don't care what anybody else says!"

"Does she indeed speak the truth?" Morgant asked.

When Taran did not answer, Morgant nodded slowly and continued in a thoughtful tone. "I believe she does, though you stay silent. There was much of Prince Ellidyr's tale which rang false to me. As I once told you, Taran of Caer Dallben, I am a warrior and I know my men. But when you face Ellidyr himself, I shall know beyond all doubt.

"Come," said Morgant, helping Taran to his steed, "we shall ride to my camp. Your task is ended. The Crochan is in my hands."

Morgant's warriors took up the rest of the companions and they galloped swiftly into the wood. The war lord had made camp in a wide clearing, well protected by trees, its approach guarded by a deep ravine, and the tents had been blended in with a line of underbrush. Taran saw Lluagor and Melynlas tethered among the steeds of the warriors; a little apart, Islimach pawed the ground nervously and pulled at her halter.

Near the center of the clearing Taran caught his breath at the sight of the Black Crochan, which now had been removed from its sling. Though two of Morgant's warriors stood by it with drawn swords, Taran could not shake off the sense of fear and foreboding that hung like a dark mist about the cauldron.

"Do you not fear Arawn will attack you here and gain the cauldron once again?" Taran whispered.

Morgant's eyes hooded over and he gave Taran a glance both of anger and pride. "Whoever challenges me shall be met," he said coldly, "be it the Lord of Annuvin himself."

A warrior drew aside the curtain of one of the pavilions, and the war lord led them inside.

There, bound hand and foot, lay the still form of Ellidyr. His face was covered with blood and he appeared so grievously battered that Eilonwy could not stifle a cry of pity.

"How is this?" Taran exclaimed, turning to Morgant in shock and reproach. "Sire," he added quickly, "your warriors had no right to use him so ill! This is shameful and dishonorable treatment."

"Do you question my conduct?" Morgant replied. "You have much to learn of obedience. My warriors heed my orders and so shall you. Prince Ellidyr dared to resist me. I caution you not to follow his example."

At a call from Morgant, armed guards strode quickly into the tent. The war-leader made a brief gesture toward Taran and his companions.

"Disarm them and bind them fast."

CHAPTER NINETEEN

The War Lord

Before the startled Taran could draw his blade, a guard seized him and quickly lashed his arms behind his back. The bard, too, was seized. Screaming and kicking, Eilonwy fought vainly. For an instant Gurgi broke loose from his captors and flung himself toward King Morgant. But a warrior struck him brutally to the ground, leaped astride the limp figure, and trussed him tightly.

"Traitor!" Eilonwy shrieked. "Liar! You dare to steal . . ."

"Silence her," Morgant said coldly, and in another moment a gag muffled her cries.

Frantically Taran struggled to reach the girl's side, before he was thrown down and his legs secured with thongs. Morgant watched silently, his features fixed and without expression. The guards stepped away from the helpless companions. Morgant gestured for the warriors to leave the tent.

Taran, whose head still spun with confusion and disbelief, strained against his bonds. "You are already a traitor," he cried. "Will you now be a murderer? We are under the protection of Gwydion; you will not escape his wrath!"

"I do not fear Gwydion," answered Morgant, "and his protection is worthless to you now. Worthless, indeed, to all Prydain. Even Gwydion is powerless against the Cauldron-Born."

Taran stared at him in horror. "You would not dare to use the Crochan against your own kinsmen, your own people. This is even more foul than treachery and murder!"

"Do you believe so?" Morgant replied. "Then you have more lessons to learn than that of obedience. The cauldron belongs to him who knows how to keep it and how to use it. It is a weapon ready for a hand. For years Arawn was master of the cauldron, yet he lost it. Is this not proof he was unworthy, that he did not have the strength or cunning to prevent its slipping from his grasp? Ellidyr, the proud fool, believed he could keep it. He is hardly fit to be cast into it."

"What," Taran cried, "will you set yourself to rival Arawn?"

"To rival him?" Morgant asked with a hard smile. "No. To sur-pass him. I know my worth, though I have chafed in the service of lesser men than I. Now I see the moment is ripe. There are few," he continued haughtily, "who understand the uses of power. And few who dare use it when it is offered them.

"Power such as this was offered once to Gwydion," Morgant went on. "He refused it. I shall not fail to take it. Shall you?"

"I?" asked Taran, with a terrified glance at Morgant.

King Morgant nodded. His eyes were hooded, but his falcon's face was keen and avid. "Gwydion has spoken of you," he said. "He told me little, but that little is of interest. You are a bold youth—and perhaps more than that. How much more, I do not know. But I do know you are without family, without name or future. You can expect nothing. And yet," Morgant added, "you can expect everything.

"I would not offer this to one such as Ellidyr," Morgant continued. "He is too prideful, weakest where he believes himself strong. Do you remember I told you that I know good mettle? There is much that is possible with you, Taran of Caer Dallben. And this is what I offer—swear that you shall serve me as your liege lord and when the time is right you shall be my war-leader, second only to me in all Prydain."

"Why do you offer me this?" Taran cried. "Why should you choose me?"

"As I have said," Morgant answered, "there is much you might achieve, if the way is opened for you. Do not deny you have dreamed long of glory. It is not impossible for you to find it, if I judge you well."

"Judge me well," Taran flung back, "and you would know I scorn to serve an evil traitor!"

"I have no time to hear you vent your rage," Morgant said. "Many plans must be made between now and dawn. I shall leave you with this to consider: will you be first among my warriors—or first among my Cauldron-Born?"

"Give me to the cauldron, then!" Taran shouted. "Cast me in it now, even as I live!"

"You have called me traitor," Morgant answered, smiling. "Do not call me fool. I, too, know the secret of the cauldron. Do you think I would have the Crochan shatter even before it began its work? Yes," he went on, "I, too, have been to the Marshes of Morva, long before the cauldron was taken from Annuvin. For I knew that sooner or later Gwydion must make this move against Arawn. And so I prepared myself. Did you pay a price for the Crochan? I, too, paid a price for the knowledge of its workings. I know how to destroy it, and I know how to make it yield a harvest of power.

"But you were bold, nonetheless, to hope to trick me," Morgant added. "You fear me," he said, drawing closer to Taran, "and there are many in Prydain who do. Yet you defy me. To dare that, there are few. This is rare metal indeed, ready to be tempered."

Taran was about to speak, but the war lord raised his hand. "Say no more. Instead, think carefully. If you refuse, you shall become a voiceless, mindless slave, without even hope of death to release you from your bondage."

Taran's heart sank, but he raised his head proudly. "If that is the destiny laid on me . . ."

"It will be a harder destiny than you believe," Morgant said, his eyes flickering. "A warrior does not fear to give up his own life. But will he sacrifice that of his comrades?"

Taran gasped with horror as Morgant went on.

"Yes," said the war lord, "one by one your companions shall be slain and given to the Crochan. Who will it devour before you cry a halt? Will it be the bard? Or the shabby creature that serves you? Or the young Princess? They shall go before you, even as you watch. And, at the last, yourself.

"Weigh this carefully," said the war lord. "I shall return for your answer." He flung his black cloak about his shoulders and strode from the tent.

Taran struggled against his bonds, but they held firm. He sank back and bowed his head.

The bard, who had been silent this while, heaved a sorrowful sigh. "In the Marshes of Morva," he said, "if I had only known, I should have asked Orddu to change me into a toad. At the time I didn't care for the idea. As I think of it now, it's a happier life than being a Cauldron warrior. At least there would have been dew circles to dance in."

"He will not succeed in this," Taran said. "Somehow, we must find a way to escape. We dare not lose hope."

"I agree absolutely," Fflewddur answered. "Your general idea is excellent; it's only the details that are lacking. Lose hope? By no means! A Fflam is always hopeful! I intend to go on hoping," he added ruefully, "even when they come and pop me into the Crochan."

Gurgi and Ellidyr still lay unconscious, but Eilonwy had not ceased working furiously at the gag and now at last she succeeded in forcing it out of her mouth.

"Morgant!" she gasped. "He'll pay for this! Why, I thought I'd stifle! He might have kept me from talking, but he didn't keep me from listening. When he comes back, I hope he tries to put me in the cauldron first! He'll soon find out who he's dealing with. He'll wish he'd never thought of making his own Cauldron-Born!"

Taran shook his head. "By then it will be too late. We shall be slain before we are taken to the Crochan. No, there is only one hope. None of you shall be sacrificed because of me. I have decided what I must do."

"Decided!" Eilonwy burst out. "The only thing you have to decide is how we shall escape from this tent. If you're thinking of anything else, you're wasting your time. That's like wondering whether to scratch your head when a boulder's about to fall on it."

"This is my decision," Taran said slowly. "I will accept what Morgant offers."

"What?" Eilonwy exclaimed in disbelief. "For a while I thought you'd actually learned something from Adaon's brooch. How can you think to accept?"

"I shall swear my allegiance to Morgant," Taran went on. "He shall have my word, but shall not make me keep it. An oath given under threat of death cannot bind me. This way, at least, we may gain a little time."

"Are you sure Morgant's warriors didn't strike you on the head and you didn't notice it?" Eilonwy asked sharply. "Do you imagine Morgant won't guess what you plan? He has no intention of keeping his part of the bargain; he'll slay us all anyway. Once you're in his clutches—I mean more than you are—you won't get out of them. Morgant might have been one of the greatest war-leaders in Prydain; but he's turned evil, and if you try coming to terms with him, well, you'll find it's worse than being a Cauldron warrior. Though I admit that isn't very attractive either."

Taran was silent for a time. "I fear you are right," he said. "But I don't know what else we can do."

"Get out first," Eilonwy advised. "We can decide what else when the time comes. Somehow it's hard to think about where to run as long as your hands and feet are tied up."

With much difficulty, the tightly bound companions struggled closer and sought to undo each other's thongs. The knots refused to yield, slipped from their numb fingers, and only bit more deeply into their flesh.

Again and again the companions returned to their labors until they lay breathless and exhausted. Even Eilonwy no longer had the strength to speak. They rested a while, hoping to gain new energy, but the night moved as a heavy, tormented dream and the moments they passed in fitful drowsing did nothing to restore them, nor did they dare lose too much precious time; morning, Taran knew, would come swiftly. The cold, gray trickle of dawn had already begun to seep into the tent.

All night, as they had toiled, Taran had heard the movements of warriors in the clearing, the voice of Morgant crying harsh, urgent commands. Now he dragged himself painfully to the curtain at the entrance of the tent, pressed his cheek against the cold ground, and tried to peer out. He could see little, for the rising mists swirled above the turf, and he made out only shadow shapes hastening back and forth. The warriors, he imagined, were gathering their gear, perhaps making ready to strike camp. A long, pitiful whinny came from the line of tethered horses and he recognized it as that of Islimach. The Crochan still squatted where it had been; Taran made out the dark, brooding mass, and it seemed to him, in a flare of horror, that its mouth gaped greedily.

Taran rolled over and pulled himself back to the companions. The bard's features were pale; he appeared half-dazed by fatigue and suffering. Eilonwy raised her head and looked silently at him.

"What," murmured Fflewddur, "has the moment already come for us to say farewell?"

"Not yet," Taran said, "though Morgant will be here soon enough, I fear. Then our time will be upon us. How does Gurgi fare?"

"The poor thing is still unconscious," Eilonwy answered. "Leave him as he is, it is kinder thus."

Ellidyr stirred and groaned feebly. Slowly his eyes opened; he winced, turned his bloodstained, broken face to Taran, and studied him for a time as though without recognition. Then his torn lips moved in his familiar, bitter grimace.

"And so we are together again, Taran of Caer Dallben," he said. "I did not expect us to meet so soon."

"Have no fear, Son of Pen-Llarcau," Taran answered. "It shall not be for long."

Ellidyr bowed his head. "For that I am truly sorry. I would make up the ill I have done all of you."

"Would you have said the same if the cauldron were still in your hands?" Taran asked quietly.

Ellidyr hesitated. "I shall speak the truth—I do not know. The black beast you saw is a harsh master; its claws are sharp. Yet I did not feel them until now.

"But I tell you this," Ellidyr continued, trying to lift himself, "I stole the cauldron out of pride, not evil. I swear to you, on whatever honor remains to me, I would not have used it. Yes, I would have taken your glory for my own. But I, too, would have borne the Crochan to Gwydion and offered it for destruction. Believe this much of me."

Taran nodded. "I believe you, Prince of Pen-Llarcau. And now perhaps even more than you believe it yourself."

A wind had risen, moaning through the trees and shaking the tent. The curtain blew back. Taran saw the warriors forming in ranks behind the cauldron.

CHAPTER TWENTY

The Final Price

"Ellidyr!" Taran cried. "Have you strength enough to break your bonds and free the rest of us?"

Ellidyr rolled on his side and strained desperately against the tight cords. The bard and Taran tried to aid him, but at last Ellidyr fell back, exhausted and gasping with the pain of his efforts.

"Too much of my strength is gone," he murmured. "I fear Morgant has given me my death wound. I can do no more."

The curtain blew open again. An instant later Taran was flung full length and roughly spun around. He kicked wildly with his bound legs and tried to right himself.

"Stop struggling, you clot!" a voice shouted in his ear.

"Doli!" Taran's heart leaped. "Is it you?"

"Clever question!" snapped the voice. "Stop trying to fight me! Things are hard enough without your squirming! Whoever tied these knots, I wish he had them about his neck!"

Taran felt firm hands drawing at the thongs. "Doli! How did you come here?"

"Don't bother me with silly chatter," growled the dwarf. Taran felt a knee jabbing into the small of his back as Doli took a better grip on the bonds. "Can't you see I'm busy?" muttered the dwarf.

"No, of course you can't, but that doesn't matter. Drat! If I hadn't lost my axe I'd be through this in no time! Oh, my ears! I've never stayed invisible so long at one go! Hornets! Wasps!"

Suddenly the thongs parted. Taran sat up and began as best he could to unbind his legs. In another moment Doli himself flashed into sight and set about freeing the bard. The stout dwarf was grimy, muddy, and his ears were tinged bright blue. Doli stopped his exertions to clap his hands to his head. "Enough invisibility is enough!" he cried. "No need for it here. Not yet. Bumblebees! A whole hive of them in my ears!"

"How did you ever find us?" cried Eilonwy, as the dwarf ripped away her bonds.

"If you must know," the dwarf snapped impatiently, "I didn't find you. Not at first. I found Ellidyr. Saw him come up from the river a little before Morgant reached him. I was on my way to Caer Cadarn, after I shook off the Huntsmen, to get help from Gwydion. I didn't dare waste time chasing through the Marshes after you. Ellidyr had the cauldron. And your horses, too. That got my suspicions up. So I went invisible and followed him on foot. As soon as I understood what had happened, I turned back to look for you. My pony had run off—dratted beast, we never liked each other—and you got here ahead of me."

The dwarf knelt and untied Gurgi, who had begun to show some signs of life, but hesitated when he came to Ellidyr. "What about this one?" Doli asked. "I have an idea he's better off as he is," he added gruffly. "I know what he tried to do."

Ellidyr raised his head.

Taran met his glance and gestured quickly to Doli. "Free him," Taran ordered.

Doli paused, doubtful. Taran repeated his words. The dwarf shook his head, then shrugged. "If you say so," he muttered, setting to work on Ellidyr's bonds.

While Eilonwy chafed Gurgi's wrists, the bard hurried to the tent flap and cautiously peered out. Taran searched vainly for weapons.

"I can see Morgant," Fflewddur called. "He's on his way here. Well, he shall have a surprise."

"We are unarmed!" Taran cried. "They far outnumber us and can slay us at their pleasure!"

"Rip up the back of the tent!" Doli exclaimed. "Make a run for it through the forest!"

"And leave the Crochan in Morgant's hands?" replied Taran. "No, that we dare not do!"

Ellidyr had risen to his feet. "I had not strength enough to break my own bonds," he said, "but I can still serve you."

Before Taran could stop him, Ellidyr plunged from the tent. The guards shouted the alarm. Taran saw Morgant fall back in astonishment, then draw his sword.

"Slay him!" Morgant commanded. "Slay him! Keep him from the cauldron!"

With the bard and Doli at his heels, Taran raced from the tent and flung himself against King Morgant, fighting furiously to wrest the sword from the war lord's hands. With a savage snarl, Morgant caught him by the throat and tossed him to the ground, then turned to pursue Ellidyr. The horsemen had broken ranks and hastened to close upon the running figure.

Taran scrambled to his feet. Ahead, he saw Ellidyr grappling fiercely with one of the warriors. Fighting as he had never fought before, the Prince of Pen-Llarcau, Taran knew, was calling on all the strength remaining to him. Ellidyr threw the warrior down, but faltered and cried out as the man's sword thrust deep into his side. Clutching the wound, Ellidyr stumbled ahead.

"No! No!" Taran shouted. "Ellidyr! Save yourself!"

A few paces from the cauldron, struggling madly, Ellidyr broke free of the warriors. Then, with a cry, he flung himself into the Crochan's gaping mouth.

The Crochan shuddered like a living thing. In horror and dismay, Taran cried out again to Ellidyr. He fought his way toward the cauldron, but in another instant a sharp clap, louder than thunder, rang above the clearing. The leafless trees trembled to their roots; the branches writhed as if in agony. Then, while echoes ripped the air and a whirlwind screamed overhead, the cauldron split and shattered. The jagged shards fell away from the lifeless form of Ellidyr.

A war horse burst from the thicket. Astride it rode King Smoit, a naked sword in his fist, a shout of battle on his lips. Behind the red-bearded King streamed mounted warriors, who plunged against the men of Morgant. In the press of combat, Taran glimpsed a white steed galloping to the charge.

"Gwydion!" Taran shouted and struggled to reach his side. He caught sight of Coll, then; the stout old warrior had drawn his sword and struck mightily about him. Gwystyl, with Kaw clinging to his shoulder, dashed into the fray.

Bellowing with rage, King Smoit drove straight for Morgant, who raised his sword and lashed viciously at the rearing steed. Smoit leaped to the ground. Two of Morgant's warriors threw themselves in front of him to defend their lord, but Smoit cut them down with powerful blows and strode past.

Eyes unhooded and blazing, his teeth bared, Morgant fought savagely amid the shattered pieces of the cauldron, as though he sought defiantly to claim them. His sword had broken under the force of Smoit's attack, yet he slashed and thrust again and again with the jagged blade, the grimace of hatred and arrogance frozen upon his features, his hand still clutching the bloodstained weapon even as he fell.

Morgant's riders had been slain or captured as Gwydion's voice rose in command to cease the combat. Taran stumbled to Ellidyr's side and tried to raise him. He bowed his head in grief. "The black beast is gone from you, Prince of Pen-Llarcau," he murmured.

A high-pitched whinny behind him made Taran turn. It was Islimach who had broken her tether and now stood over the body of her master. The roan lifted her lean, bony head, tossed her mane, spun about, and galloped from the clearing.

Taran, understanding the frenzied look in the roan's eyes, cried out and ran after her. Islimach plunged through the undergrowth. Taran strove to overtake her and seize the hanging bridle, but the roan sped onward to the ravine. She did not check her speed even at the brink. Islimach made a mighty leap, hung poised in the air a moment, then plummeted to the rocks below. Taran covered his face with his hands and turned away.

In the clearing the bodies of King Morgant and Ellidyr lay side by side, and the remainder of King Smoit's horsemen rode in a slow, mournful circle around them. Alone and apart, Gwydion leaned heavily on the black sword Dyrnwyn, his shaggy head bent, his weathered face filled with sorrow. Taran drew near and stood silently.

At length Gwydion spoke. "Fflewddur has told me all that befell you. My heart is grieved that Coll and I found you only now. Yet, without King Smoit and his warriors, I fear we might not have prevailed. He grew impatient and came seeking us. Had I been able to send him word, I would have summoned him long before this. I am grateful to him for his impatience.

"And to you, too, Assistant Pig-Keeper," he added. "The Crochan is destroyed, and with it Arawn's power to add to the number of his Cauldron-Born. It is one of the gravest defeats Arawn has ever suffered. But I know the price you paid."

"It is Ellidyr who paid the final price," Taran said slowly. "The last honor belongs to him." He spoke then of Islimach. "He has lost all else, even his steed."

"Or perhaps gained all," Gwydion answered. "And his honor shall be certain. We shall raise a barrow to his memory. Islimach, too, shall rest with him, for they are both now at peace. Smoit's dead shall also sleep in honor, and a barrow be raised above Morgant King of Madoc."

"Morgant?" Taran asked, turning a puzzled glance to Gwydion. "How can there be honor for such a man?"

"It is easy to judge evil unmixed," replied Gwydion. "But, alas, in most of us good and bad are closely woven as the threads on a loom; greater wisdom than mine is needed for the judging.

"King Morgant served the Sons of Don long and well," he went on. "Until the thirst for power parched his throat, he was a fearless and noble lord. In battle he saved my life more than once. These things are part of him and cannot be put aside or forgotten.

"And so shall I honor Morgant," Gwydion said, "for what he used to be, and Ellidyr Prince of Pen-Llarcau for what he became."

❖

Near the tents of Morgant, Taran found the companions again. Under Eilonwy's care, Gurgi had recovered from the guard's blow and looked only a little shaken.

"Poor tender head is filled with breakings and achings," Gurgi said, with a wan smile at Taran. "He is sad not to fight at side of kindly master. He would have struck down wicked warriors, oh, yes!"

"There's been more than enough fighting," Eilonwy said. "I found your sword again," she added, handing the weapon to Taran. "But sometimes I wish Dallben hadn't given it to you in the first place. It's bound to lead to trouble."

"Oh, I should think our troubles are over," put in Fflewddur, cradling his injured arm. "The beastly old kettle is smashed to bits, thanks to Ellidyr," he went on sadly. "The bards shall sing of our deeds—and of his."

"I don't care about that," grumbled Doli, rubbing his ears, which had only now begun to return to their natural color. "I just don't want anyone, not even Gwydion, dreaming up another scheme to have me turn invisible."

"Good old Doli," Taran said. "The more you grumble, the more pleased you are with yourself."

"Good old Doli," replied the dwarf. "Humph!"

Taran caught sight of Coll and King Smoit resting beneath an oak. Coll had taken off his close-fitting helmet and, though bruised and slashed, his face beamed and his bald head glowed with plea- sure, as he put an arm around Taran's shoulders. "We did not meet as soon as I expected," Coll said with a wink, "for I hear you were busy with other things."

"My body and blood!" roared Smoit, giving Taran a clap on the back. "You looked like a skinned rabbit last time I saw you. Now the rabbit is gone and only the skin and bones are left!"

A loud squawk interrupted the red-bearded King. In surprise Taran turned and saw Gwystyl, sitting alone and morose. On his shoulder Kaw hopped up and down and bobbed his head in delight.

"So it's you again," Gwystyl remarked, sighing heavily as Taran hurried over. "Well, you shan't blame me for what's happened. I warned you. However, what's done is done and there's no sense complaining. No use in it at all."

"You shall not deceive me again, Gwystyl of the Fair Folk," Taran said. "I know who you are and the valiant service you have rendered."

Kaw croaked joyfully as Taran smoothed his feathers and scratched him under the beak.

"Go on," Gwystyl said, "put him on your shoulder. That's what he wants. For the matter of that, you shall have him as a gift, with the thanks of the Fair Folk. For you have done us a service, too. We were uneasy with the Crochan knocking about here and there; one never knew what would happen. Yes, yes, pick him up," Gwystyl added with a melancholy sigh. "He's taken quite a fancy to you. It's just as well. I'm simply not up to keeping crows any more, not up to it at all."

"Taran!" croaked Kaw.

"Though I warn you again," Gwystyl went on, "pay no attention to him. Most of the time he talks just to hear himself talk—like some others I could mention. The secret is: don't listen. No use in it. No use whatever."

❖

After they had raised the barrows, Gwystyl left to resume his guard at the way post; the companions, King Smoit, and his riders departed from the clearing and turned their horses toward the Great Avren. High overhead, their wings darkening the sky, flight after flight of gwythaints retreated toward Annuvin. Of the Huntsmen there was no sign; and Gwydion believed that Arawn, learning of the Crochan's destruction, had summoned them to return.

The companions rode not in triumphant joy but slowly and thoughtfully. The heart of King Smoit, too, was heavy, for he had suffered the loss of many warriors.

With Kaw perched on his shoulder, Taran rode beside Gwydion at the head of the column as it wound through hills rich with autumn's colors. For a long while Taran did not speak.

"It is strange," he said at last. "I had longed to enter the world of men. Now I see it filled with sorrow, with cruelty and treachery, with those who would destroy all around them."

"Yet, enter it you must," Gwydion answered, "for it is a destiny laid on each of us. True, you have seen these things. But there are equal parts of love and joy. Think of Adaon and believe this.

"Think, too, of your companions. Out of friendship for you, they would have given up all they valued; indeed, all they possessed."

Taran nodded. "I see now the price I paid was the least of all, for the brooch was never truly mine. I wore it, but it was not part of me. I am thankful I kept it as long as I did; at least I knew, for a little while, how a bard must feel and what it must be like to be a hero."

"That is why your sacrifice was all the more difficult," Gwydion said. "You chose to be a hero not through enchantment but through your own manhood. And since you have chosen, for good or ill, you must take the risks of a man. You may win or you may lose. Time will decide."

They had come into the Valley of Ystrad, and here Gwydion reined up the golden-maned steed.

"Melyngar and I must now return to Caer Dathyl," he said, "and bring word to King Math. You shall tell Dallben all that has happened; indeed, this time you know more of these events than I.

"Go swiftly," Gwydion said, reaching out his hand. "Your comrades wait for you; and Coll, I know, is eager to ready his vegetable garden for winter. Farewell, Taran, Assistant Pig-Keeper—and friend."

Gwydion waved once and rode northward. Taran watched until he was out of sight. He turned Melynlas, then, and saw the faces of the companions smiling at him.

"Hurry along," Eilonwy called. "Hen Wen will be wanting her bath. And I'm afraid Gurgi and I left in such a hurry I didn't take time to straighten up the scullery. That's worse than starting a journey and forgetting to put on your shoes!"

Taran galloped toward them.

Turn the page for

The Black Cauldron

bonus materials. . . .

Prydain Pronunciation Guide

✣

Achren AHK-*ren*

Adaon *ah*-DAY-*on*

Aeddan EE-*dan*

Angharad *an*-GAR-*ad*

Annuvin *ah*-NOO-*vin*

Arawn *ah*-RAWN

Arianllyn *ahree*-AHN-*lin*

Briavael *bree*-AH-*vel*

Brynach BRIHN-*ak*

Caer Cadarn *kare* KAH-*darn*

Caer Colur *kare* KOH-*loor*

Caer Dathyl *kare* DA-*thil*

Coll *kahl*

Dallben DAHL-*ben*

Doli DOH-*lee*

Don *dahn*

Dwyvach DWIH-*vak*

Dyrnwyn DUHRN-*win*

Edyrnion *eh*-DIR-*nyon*

Eiddileg *eye*-DILL-*eg*

Eilonwy *eye*-LAHN-*wee*

Ellidyr ELLI-*deer*

Fflewddur Fflam FLEW-*der flam*

Geraint GHER-*aint*

Goewin GOH-*win*

Govannion *go*-VAH-*nyon*

Gurgi GHER-*ghee*

Gwydion GWIH-*dyon*

Gwythaint GWIH-*thaint*

Islimach *iss*-LIM-*ahk*

Llawgadarn *law*-GAD-*arn*

Lluagor *lew*-AH-*gore*

Llunet LOO-*net*

Llyan *lee*-AHN

Llyr *leer*

Melyngar MELLIN-*gar*

Melynlas MELLIN-*lass*

Oeth-Anoeth *eth*-AHN-*eth*

Orddu   OR-*doo*
Orgoch   OR-*gahk*
Orwen   OR-*wen*

Prydain   *prih-DANE*
Pryderi   *prih-DAY-ree*

Rhuddlum   ROOD-*lum*
Rhun   *roon*

Smoit   *smoyt*

Taliesin   *tally-ESS-in*
Taran   TAH-*ran*
Teleria   *tell-EHR-ya*

11 September, 1964
3847 Dennison Avenue
Drexel Hill, Pa.

Dear Ann:

OK, here it is back again. Most of the dandelions
have been weeded out, but Louise will probably find more!
A lot of the pages have been retyped -- ones either rewritten
or starting to look messy with corrections -- so in some
cases your marginal notes aren't there. (I do have the old
pages with your notes if you want them.) But all your
questions have been answered and all the revisions made
as we discussed.

Hope you like the new opening, page 1. You're right,
the original opening paragraphs just weren't right. These
may be a little better. Throughout the first chapter, I've
also worked in the other points you wanted established --
Dallben being the most powerful enchanter in Prydain,
Eilonwy obviously working in the scullery; and, during
the council, the comment that evil is never distant, etc.
Have also worked in King Math here and there (damn him!
since I'm stuck with him, some day I might as well make
a real character out of him!).

Adaon, I hope, now emerges as a more complete character. I've rewritten and expanded his scenes, especially
on pages 9-10, 21, 27through 30, 84-85, plus a few little
things here and there. He now has a most interesting past,
and a very bright and promising future -- and I hope everybody weeps!

Have also worked on Orwen. She now not only has a nice
peculiar necklace to play with, but I've reworked much of
her dialogue and she's now quite different from the others;
she's more, excuse the expression, girlish and eager!

Have also fixed up other little things here and there,
as they occurred to me looking at the pages again.

So -- hope you like the result. If not, holler. As
I said, some of those seemingly innocent comments of yours

A letter from Lloyd Alexander to his editor at Henry Holt, Ann Durell, sent with a draft of
The Black Cauldron.

were harder to answer than you might think. But I'm
delighted. Working out the answers almost automatically
strengthened the book. As usual, I only wish I'd thought
of them before!

The bane of my existence, the NOTE, will be forth-
coming very shortly. Having struggled through the first,
the second shouldn't be as hard.   ???

Exhaustedly,

Lloyd

10 November, 1964
3847 Dennison Avenue
Drexel Hill, Pa.

Dear Ann:

Here is the Cauldron back again. The questions have
been answered, the suggestions incorporated, with a few
exceptions noted on the attached.

I've also included, if you want to use it, a new
first paragraph for the Author's Note. You'd mentioned
(I _think_ you did, when we talked on the phone) revising
it to delete reference to The Book of Three. Think the
new version will do.

Your suggestions about Adaon's betrothed worked
perfectly and made things even more heartbreaking. In
the passage where he, in effect, makes his will, I was
stumped for a while, figuring he should leave her something
valuable (he obviously wouldn't leave her his horse, etc.).
But I think this does it -- by making his betrothed the
one who gave him the brooch in the first place!

The speech about greater honor in a field well plowed
seemed# to fit just right on page 199, giving a good end
to that particular scene.

So -- unless something drastic occurs to you -- I
guess it's ready. Pass on my gratitude to Louise, and my
sympathy for having to cope with grammar and punctuation
that often are peculiar, to say the least. Yet, it _seems_
right when I do it.

All best,

Lloyd

Letter from Lloyd Alexander to Ann Durell, probably sent with the final draft of
The Black Cauldron.

30 January, 1966
3847 Dennison Avenue
Drexel Hill, Pa.

Dear Ann:

Welcome back from Chicago! Right after you called
with THE NEWS it began snowing, it has been snowing just
about ever since, there are now ten inches around the
house. Orgoch, you see, had promised me a warm day for
my birthday but she -- even she -- got so excited she
got everything backwards. So I have just been sitting
around looking smug and insufferable.

Anyhow, you can imagine how delighted I am. And
very touched that you called. I still say writing is
the easy part. What you have to cope with is consid-
erably tougher; and, as always, you know I'm deeply
appreciative.

One advantage of this blizzard, I've got some
work done. There's nothing else to do! I can't even
get out to celebrate!

Best from Janine and the cats who (the cats,
not Janine) are pretending to be Abominable Snowmen.

See you soon,

Lloyd

Letter from Lloyd Alexander to Ann Durell. "THE NEWS" refers to the news that he had
received a Newbery Honor for *The Black Cauldron*. The American Library Association
conference, where the Newbery Medal and Honor books are announced, was held in Chicago
that year.

The Foundling

A story from

The Foundling
and Other Tales of Prydain

by
Lloyd Alexander

This is told of Dallben, greatest of enchanters in Prydain: how three black-robed hags found him, when he was still a baby, in a basket at the edge of the Marshes of Morva. "Oh, Orddu, see what's here!" cried the one named Orwen, peering into the wicker vessel floating amid the tall grasses. "Poor lost duckling! He'll catch his death of cold! Whatever shall we do with him?"

"A sweet morsel," croaked the one named Orgoch from the depths of her hood. "A tender lamb. I know what I should do."

"Please be silent, Orgoch," said the one named Orddu. "You've already had your breakfast." Orddu was a short, plump woman with a round, lumpy face and sharp black eyes. Jewels, pins, and brooches glittered in her tangle of weedy hair. "We can't leave him here to get all soggy. I suppose we shall have to take him home with us."

"Oh, yes!" exclaimed Orwen, dangling her string of milky white beads over the tiny figure in the basket. "Ah, the darling tadpole! Look at his pink cheeks and chubby little fingers! He's smiling at us, Orddu! He's waving! But what shall we call him? He mustn't go bare and nameless."

"If you ask me—" began Orgoch.

"No one did," replied Orddu. "You are quite right, Orwen. We must give him a name. Otherwise, how shall we know who he is?"

"We have so many names lying around the cottage," said Orwen. "Some of them never used. Give him a nice, fresh, unwrinkled one."

"There's a charming name I'd been saving for a special occasion," Orddu said, "but I can't remember what I did with it. No matter. His name—his name: Dallben."

"Lovely!" cried Orwen, clapping her hands. "Oh, Orddu, you have such good taste."

"Taste, indeed!" snorted Orgoch. "Dallben? Why call him Dallben?"

"Why not?" returned Orddu. "It will do splendidly. Very good quality, very durable. It should last him a lifetime."

"It will last him," Orgoch muttered, "as long as he needs it."

And so Dallben was named and nursed by these three, and given a home in their cottage near the Marshes of Morva. Under their care he grew sturdy, bright, and fair of face. He was kind and generous, and each day handsomer and happier.

The hags did not keep from him that he was a foundling. But when he was of an age to wonder about such matters, he asked where indeed he had come from, and what the rest of the world was like.

"My dear chicken," replied Orddu, "as to where you came from, we haven't the slightest notion. Nor, might I say, the least interest. You're here with us now, to our delight, and that's quite enough to know."

"As to the rest of the world," Orwen added, "don't bother your pretty, curly head about it. You can be sure it doesn't bother about you. Be glad you were found instead of drowned. Why, this very moment you might be part of a school of fish. And what a slippery, scaly sort of life that would be!"

"I like fish," muttered Orgoch, "especially eels."

"Do hush, dear Orgoch," said Orddu. "You're always thinking of your stomach."

Despite his curiosity, Dallben saw there was no use in questioning further. Cheerful and willing, he went about every task with eagerness and good grace. He drew pails of water from the well, kept the fire burning in the hearth, pumped the bellows, swept away the ashes, and dug the garden. No toil was too troublesome for him. When Orddu spun thread, he turned the spinning wheel. He helped Orwen measure the skeins into lengths and held them for Orgoch to snip with a pair of rusty shears.

One day, when the three brewed a potion of roots and herbs, Dallben was left alone to stir the huge, steaming kettle with a long iron spoon. He obeyed the hags' warning not to taste the liquid, but soon the potion began boiling so briskly that a few drops bubbled up and by accident splashed his fingers. With a cry of pain, Dallben let fall the spoon and popped his fingers into his mouth.

His outcry brought Orddu, Orwen, and Orgoch hurrying back to the cottage.

"Oh, the poor sparrow!" gasped Orwen, seeing the boy sucking at his blistered knuckles. "He's gone and burned himself. I'll fetch an ointment for the sweet fledgling, and some spiderwebs to bandage him. What did you do with all those spiders, Orgoch? They were here only yesterday."

"Too late for all that," growled Orgoch. "Worse damage is done."

"Yes, I'm afraid so," Orddu sighed. "There's no learning without pain. The dear gosling has had his pain; and now, I daresay, he has some learning to go along with it."

Dallben, meanwhile, had swallowed the drops of liquid scalding his fingers. He licked his lips at the taste, sweet and bitter at the same time. And in that instant he began to shake with fear and excitement. All that had been common and familiar in the cottage he saw as he had never seen before.

Now he understood that the leather bellows lying by the hearth commanded the four winds; the pail of water in the corner, the seas and oceans of the world. The earthen floor of the cottage held the roots of all plants and trees. The fire showed him the secrets of its flame, and how all things come to ashes. He gazed awe-struck at the enchantresses, for such they were.

"The threads you spin, and measure, and cut off," Dallben murmured, "these are no threads, but the lives of men. I know who you truly are."

"Oh, I doubt it," Orddu cheerfully answered. "Even we aren't always sure of that. Nevertheless, one taste of that magical brew and you know as much as we do. Almost as much, at any rate."

"Too much for his own good," muttered Orgoch.

"But what shall we do?" moaned Orwen. "He was such a sweet, innocent little robin. If only he hadn't swallowed the potion! Is there no way to make him unswallow it?"

"We could try," said Orgoch.

"No," declared Orddu. "What's done is done. You know that as well as I. Alas, the dear duckling will have to leave us. There's nothing else for it. So many people, knowing so much, under the same roof? All that knowledge crammed in, crowded, bumping and jostling back and forth? We'd not have room to breathe!"

"I say he should be kept," growled Orgoch.

"I don't think he'd like your way of keeping him," Orddu answered. She turned to Dallben. "No, my poor chicken, we must say farewell. You asked us once about the world? I'm afraid you'll have to see it for yourself."

"But, Orddu," protested Orwen, "we can't let him march off just like that. Surely we have some little trinket he'd enjoy? A going-away present, so he won't forget us?"

"I could give him something to remember us by," began Orgoch.

"No doubt," said Orddu. "But that's not what Orwen had in mind. Of course, we shall offer him a gift. Better yet, he shall choose one for himself."

As Dallben watched, the enchantress unlocked an iron-bound chest and rummaged inside, flinging out all sorts of oddments until there was a large heap on the floor.

"Here's something," Orddu at last exclaimed. "Just the thing for a bold young chicken. A sword!"

Dallben caught his breath in wonder as Orddu put the weapon in his hands. The hilt, studded with jewels, glittered so brightly that he was dazzled and nearly blinded. The blade flashed, and a thread of fire ran along its edges.

"Take this, my duckling," Orddu said, "and you shall be the greatest warrior in Prydain. Strength and power, dear gosling! When you command, all must obey even your slightest whim."

"It is a fine blade," Dallben replied, "and comes easily to my hand."

"It shall be yours," Orddu said. "At least, as long as you're able to keep it. Oh, yes," the enchantress went on, "I should mention it's already had a number of owners. Somehow, sooner or later, it wanders back to us. The difficulty, you see, isn't so much getting power as holding on to it. Because so many others want it, too. You'd be astonished, the lengths to which some will go. Be warned, the sword can be lost or stolen. Or bent out of shape—as, indeed, so can you, in a manner of speaking."

"And remember," put in Orwen, "you must never let it out of your sight, not for an instant."

Dallben hesitated a moment, then shook his head. "I think your gift is more burden than blessing."

"In that case," Orddu said, "perhaps this will suit you better."

As Dallben laid down the sword, the enchantress handed him a golden harp, so perfectly wrought that he no sooner held it than it seemed to play of itself.

"Take this, my sparrow," said Orddu, "and be the greatest bard in Prydain, known throughout the land for the beauty of your songs."

Dallben's heart leaped as the instrument thrilled in his arms. He touched the sweeping curve of the glowing harp and ran his fingers over the golden strings. "I have never heard such music," he murmured. "Who owns this will surely have no lack of fame."

"You'll have fame and admiration a-plenty," said Orddu, "as long as anyone remembers you."

"Alas, that's true," Orwen said with a sigh. "Memory can be so skimpy. It doesn't stretch very far; and, next thing you know, there's your fame gone all crumbly and mildewed."

Sadly, Dallben set down the harp. "Beautiful it is," he said, "but in the end, I fear, little help to me."

"There's nothing else we can offer at the moment," said Orddu, delving once more into the chest, "unless you'd care to have this book."

The enchantress held up a large, heavy tome and blew away the dust and cobwebs from its moldering leather binding. "It's a bulky thing for a young lamb to carry. Naturally, it would be rather weighty, for it holds everything that was ever known, is known, and will be known."

"It's full of wisdom, thick as oatmeal," added Orwen. "Quite scarce in the world—wisdom, not oatmeal—but that only makes it the more valuable."

"We have so many requests for other items," Orddu said. "Seven-league boots, cloaks of invisibility, and such great nonsense. For wisdom, practically none. Yet whoever owns this book shall have all that and more, if he likes. For the odd thing about wisdom is the more you use it the more it grows; and the more you share, the more you gain. You'd be amazed how few understand that. If they did, I suppose, they wouldn't need the book in the first place."

"Do you give this to me?" Dallben asked. "A treasure greater than all treasures?"

Orddu hesitated. "Give? Only in a manner of speaking. If you know us as well as you say you do, then you also know we don't exactly *give* anything. Put it this way: We shall *let* you take that heavy, dusty old book if that's what you truly want. Again, be warned: The greater the treasure, the greater the cost. Nothing is given for nothing; not in the Marshes of Morva—or anyplace else, for the matter of that."

"Even so," Dallben replied, "this book is my choice."

"Very well," said Orddu, putting the ancient volume in his hands. "Now you shall be on your way. We're sorry to see you go, though sorrow is something we don't usually feel. Fare well, dear chicken. We mean this in the polite sense, for whether you fare well or ill is entirely up to you."

So Dallben took his leave of the enchantresses and set off eagerly, curious to see what lay in store not only in the world but between the covers of the book. Once the cottage was well out of sight and the marshes far behind him, he curbed his impatience no longer, but sat down by the roadside, opened the heavy tome, and began to read.

As he scanned the first pages, his eyes widened and his heart quickened. For here was knowledge he had never dreamed of: the pathways of the stars, the rounds of the planets, the ebb and flow of time and tide. All secrets of the world and all its hidden lore unfolded to him.

Dallben's head spun, giddy with delight. The huge book seemed to weigh less than a feather, and he felt so lighthearted he could have skipped from one mountaintop to the next and never touched the ground. He laughed and sang at the top of his voice, bursting with gladness, pride, and strength in what he had learned.

"I chose well!" he cried, jumping to his feet. "But why should Orddu have warned me? Cost? What cost can there be? Knowledge is joy!"

He strode on, reading as he went. Each page lightened and sped his journey, and soon he came to a village where the dwellers danced and sang and made holiday. They offered him meat and drink and shelter for the coming night.

But Dallben thanked them for their hospitality and shook his head, saying he had meat and drink enough in the book he carried. By this time he had walked many miles, but his spirit was fresh and his legs unweary.

He kept on his way, hardly able to contain his happiness as he read and resolving not to rest until he had come to the end of the book. But he had finished less than half when the pages, to his horror, began to grow dark and stained with blood and tears.

For now the book told him of other ways of the world; of cruelty, suffering, and death. He read of greed, hatred, and war; of men striving against one another with fire and sword; of the blossoming earth trampled underfoot, of harvests lost and lives cut short. And the book told that even in the same village he had passed, a day would come when no house would stand; when women would weep for their men, and children for their parents; and where they had offered him meat and drink, they would starve for lack of a crust of bread.

Each page he read pierced his heart. The book, which had seemed to weigh so little, now grew so heavy that his pace faltered and he staggered under the burden. Tears blinded his eyes, and he stumbled to the ground.

All night he lay shattered by despair. At dawn he stirred and found it took all his efforts even to lift his head. Bones aching, throat parched, he crept on hands and knees to quench his thirst from a puddle of water. There, at the sight of his reflection, he drew back and cried out in anguish.

His fair, bright curls had gone frost-white and fell below his brittle shoulders. His cheeks, once full and flushed with youth, were now hollow and wrinkled, half hidden by a long, gray beard. His brow, smooth yesterday, was scarred and furrowed, his hands gnarled and knotted, his eyes pale as if their color had been wept away.

Dallben bowed his head. "Yes, Orddu," he whispered, "I should have heeded you. Nothing is given without cost. But is the cost of wisdom so high? I thought knowledge was joy. Instead, it is grief beyond bearing."

The book lay nearby. Its last pages were still unread and, for a moment, Dallben thought to tear them to shreds and scatter them to the wind. Then he said:

"I have begun it, and I will finish it, whatever else it may foretell."

Fearfully and reluctantly, he began to read once more. But now his heart lifted. These pages told not only of death, but of birth as well; how the earth turns in its own time and in its own way gives back what is given to it; how things lost may be found again; and how one day ends for another to begin. He learned that the lives of men are short and filled with pain, yet each one a priceless treasure, whether it be that of a prince or a pig-keeper. And, at the last, the book taught him that while nothing was certain, all was possible.

"At the end of knowledge, wisdom begins," Dallben murmured. "And at the end of wisdom there is not grief, but hope."

He climbed to his withered legs and hobbled along his way, clasping the heavy book. After a time a farmer drove by in a horse-drawn cart, and called out to him:

"Come, Grandfather, ride with me if you like. That book must be a terrible load for an old man like you."

"Thank you just the same," Dallben answered, "but I have strength enough now to go to the end of my road."

"And where might that be?"

"I do not know," Dallben said. "I go seeking it."

"Well, then," said the farmer, "may you be lucky enough to find it."

"Luck?" Dallben answered. He smiled and shook his head. "Not luck, but hope. Indeed, hope."

When Eilonwy is put under a
deep spell by Queen Achren,
Taran and his companions set out on a dangerous
quest to rescue their friend. But how can a lowly
Assistant Pig-Keeper hope to stand against the
most evil enchantress in all of Prydain?

Turn the page for a sneak peek of **The Castle of Llyr**.

CHAPTER ONE

Prince Rhun

Eilonwy of the red-gold hair, the Princess Eilonwy Daughter of Angharad Daughter of Regat of the Royal House of Llyr, was leaving Caer Dallben. Dallben himself had so ordered it; and though Taran's heart was suddenly and strangely heavy, he knew there was no gainsaying the old enchanter's words.

On the spring morning set for Eilonwy's departure, Taran saddled the horses and led them from the stable. The Princess, looking desperately cheerful, had wrapped her few belongings in a small bundle slung from her shoulder. At her neck hung a fine chain and crescent moon of silver; on her finger she wore a ring of ancient craftsmanship; and in the fold of her cloak she carried another of her most prized possessions: the golden sphere that shone at her command with a light brighter than a flaming torch.

Dallben, whose face was more careworn than usual and whose back was bowed as though under a heavy burden, embraced the girl at the cottage door. "You shall always have a place in Caer Dallben," he said, "and a larger one in my heart. But, alas, raising a young lady is a mystery beyond even an enchanter's skill. I have had," he added with a quick smile, "difficulties enough raising an Assistant Pig-Keeper.

"I wish you a fair voyage to the Isle of Mona," Dallben went on. "King Rhuddlum and Queen Teleria are kindly and gracious. They are eager to stand in your family's stead and serve as your protectors, and from Queen Teleria you shall learn how a princess should behave."

"What!" cried Eilonwy. "I don't care about being a princess! And since I'm already a young lady, how else could I behave? That's like asking a fish to learn how to swim!"

"Hem!" Dallben said wryly. "I have never seen a fish with skinned knees, torn robe, and unshod feet. They would ill become him, as they ill become you." He set a gnarled hand gently on Eilonwy's shoulder. "Child, child, do you not see? For each of us comes a time when we must be more than what we are." He turned now to Taran. "Watch over her carefully," he said. "I have certain misgivings about letting you and Gurgi go with her, but if it will ease your parting, so be it."

"The Princess Eilonwy shall go safely to Mona," Taran answered.

"And you," said Dallben, "return safely. My heart will not be at ease until you do." He embraced the girl again and went quickly into the cottage.

It had been decided that Coll would accompany them to Great Avren harbor and lead back the horses. The stout old warrior, already mounted, waited patiently. Shaggy-haired Gurgi, astride his pony, looked as mournful as an owl with a stomachache. Kaw, the tame crow, perched in unwonted silence on Taran's saddle. Taran helped Eilonwy mount Lluagor, her favorite steed, then swung to the back of Melynlas, his silver-maned stallion.

Leaving Caer Dallben behind, the little band set out across the soft hills toward Avren. Side by side Taran and Coll rode ahead of the others to lead the way, Kaw meanwhile having made himself comfortable on Taran's shoulder.

"She never stopped talking for a moment," Taran said gloomily. "Now, at least, it will be quieter in Caer Dallben."

"That it will," said Coll.

"And less to worry about. She was always getting into one scrape or another."

"That, too," said Coll.

"It's for the best," Taran said. "Eilonwy is, after all, a Princess of Llyr. It's not as if she were only an Assistant Pig-Keeper."

"Very true," said Coll, looking off toward the pale hills.

They jogged along silently for a while.

"I shall miss her," Taran burst out at last, half angrily.

The old warrior grinned and rubbed his shining bald head. "Did you tell her that?"

"Not—not exactly," faltered Taran. "I suppose I should have. But every time I began talking about it I—I felt very odd. Besides, you never know what silly remark she'll come out with when you're trying to be serious."

"It may be," replied Coll, smiling, "we know least what we treasure most. But we will have more than enough to keep us busy when you come back, and you will learn, my boy, there is nothing like work to put the heart at rest."

Taran nodded sadly. "I suppose so," he said.

Past midday they turned their horses to the west, where the hills began a long slope downward into the Avren valley. At the last ridge Kaw hopped from Taran's shoulder and flapped aloft, croaking with excitement. Taran urged Melynlas over the rise. Below, the great river swung into view, wider here than he had ever seen it. Sunlight flecked the water in the sheltered curve of the harbor. A long, slender craft bobbed at the shore. Taran could make out figures aboard, hauling on ropes to raise a square, white sail.

Eilonwy and Gurgi had also ridden forward. Taran's heart leaped; and to all the companions the sight of the harbor and the waiting vessel was like a sea wind driving sorrow before it. Eilonwy began chattering gaily, and Gurgi waved his arms so wildly he nearly tumbled from the saddle.

"Yes, oh yes!" he cried. "Bold, valiant Gurgi is glad to follow kindly master and noble Princess with boatings and floatings!"

They cantered down the slope and dismounted at the water's edge. Seeing them, the sailors ran a plank out from the vessel to the shore. No sooner had they done so than a young man clambered onto the plank and hastened with eager strides toward the companions. But he had taken only a few paces along the swaying board when he lost his footing, stumbled, and with a loud splash pitched headlong into the shallows.

Taran and Coll ran to help him, but the young man had already picked himself up and was awkwardly sloshing his way ashore. He was of Taran's age, with a moon-round face, pale blue eyes, and straw-colored hair. He wore a sword and a small, richly ornamented dagger in a belt of silver links. His cloak and jacket, worked with threads of gold and silver, were now sopping wet; the stranger, however, appeared not the least dismayed either by his ducking or the sodden state of his garments. Instead, he grinned as cheerfully as if nothing whatever had befallen him.

"Hullo, hullo!" he called, waving a dripping hand. "Is that Princess Eilonwy I see? Of course! It must be!"

Without further ado, and without stopping even to wring out his cloak, he bowed so low that Taran feared the young man would lose his balance; then he straightened up and in a solemn voice declared: "On behalf of Rhuddlum Son of Rhudd and Teleria Daughter of Tannwen, King and Queen of the Isle of Mona, greetings to the Princess Eilonwy of the Royal House of Llyr, and to—well—to all the rest of you," he added, blinking rapidly as a thought suddenly occurred to him. "I should have asked your names before I started."

Taran, taken aback and not a little vexed by this scatterbrained behavior, stepped forward and presented the companions. Before he could ask the stranger's name, the young man interrupted.

"Splendid! You must all introduce yourselves again later, one at a time. Otherwise, I might forget—oh, I see the shipmaster's waving at us. Something to do with tides, no doubt. He's always very concerned with them. This is the first time I've commanded a voyage," he went on proudly. "Amazing how easy it is. All you need to do is tell the sailors . . ."

"But who are you?" Taran asked, puzzled.

The young man blinked at him. "Did I forget to mention that? I'm Prince Rhun."

"*Prince* Rhun?" Taran repeated in a tone of disbelief.

"Quite so," answered Rhun, smiling pleasantly. "King Rhuddlum's my father; and, of course, Queen Teleria's my mother. Shall we go aboard? I should hate to upset the shipmaster, for he does worry about those tides."

Coll embraced Eilonwy. "When we see you again," he told her, "I doubt we shall recognize you. You shall be a fine Princess."

"I want to be recognized!" Eilonwy cried. "I want to be me!"

"Never fear," said Coll, winking. He turned to Taran. "And you, my boy, farewell. When you return, send Kaw ahead to tell me and I shall meet you at Avren harbor."

Prince Rhun, offering his arm to Eilonwy, led her across the plank. Gurgi and Taran followed them. Having formed his own opinion of Rhun's agility, Taran kept a wary eye on the Prince until Eilonwy was safe aboard.

The ship was surprisingly roomy and well-fitted. The deck was long, with benches for oarsmen on either side. At the stern rose a high, square shed topped by a platform.

The sailors dipped their oars and worked the vessel to the middle of the river. Coll trotted along the bank and waved with all his might. The old warrior dropped from sight as the ship swung around a bend in the ever-widening river. Kaw had flapped to the masthead and, as the breeze whistled through his feathers, he beat his wings so pridefully that he looked more like a black rooster than a crow. The shore turned gray in the distance and the craft sped seaward.

If Rhun had perplexed and vaguely irritated him at their first meeting, Taran now began to wish he had never laid eyes on the Prince. Taran had meant to speak with Eilonwy apart, for there was much in his heart he longed to tell her. Yet each time he ventured to do so, Prince Rhun would pop up as if from nowhere, his round face beaming happily, calling out, "Hullo, hullo!"—a greeting Taran found more infuriating each time he heard it.

Once, the Prince of Mona eagerly dashed up to show the companions a large fish he had caught—to the delight of Eilonwy and Gurgi, but not Taran; for a moment later, Rhun's attention turned elsewhere and he hurried off, leaving Taran holding the wet, slippery fish in his arms. Another time, while leaning over the side to point out a school of dolphins, the Prince nearly dropped his sword into the sea. Luckily Taran caught it before the blade was lost forever.

After the ship reached open water Prince Rhun decided to take a hand at steering. But he no sooner grasped the tiller than it flew out of his fingers. While Rhun clutched at the wooden handle, the vessel lurched and slewed about so violently that Taran was flung against the bulwark. A water cask broke loose and went rolling down the deck, the sail flapped madly at the sudden change of course, and one bank of oars nearly snapped before the steersman regained the tiller from the undismayed Prince. The painful bump on Taran's head did nothing to raise his esteem of Prince Rhun's seamanship.

Although the Prince made no further attempt to steer the vessel, he climbed atop the platform where he called out orders to the crew.

"Lash up the sail!" Rhun shouted happily. "Steady the helm!"

No seaman himself, Taran nevertheless realized the sail was already tightly lashed and the craft was moving unwaveringly through the water; and he very shortly became aware that the sailors were quietly going about their task of keeping the ship on course without paying any heed whatever to the Prince.

Taran's head ached from the bump, his jacket was still unpleasantly damp and fishy, and when at last his chance came to speak with Eilonwy he was altogether out of sorts.

"Prince of Mona indeed!" he muttered. "He's no more than a—a princeling, a clumsy, muddle-headed baby. Commanding the voyage? If the sailors listened to him, we'd be aground in no time. I've never sailed a ship, but I've no doubt I could do it better than he. I've never seen anyone so feckless."

"Feckless?" answered Eilonwy. "He does often seem a little dense. But I'm sure he means well, and I've a feeling he has a good heart. In fact, I think he's rather nice."

"I suppose you do," Taran replied, all the more nettled by Eilonwy's words. "Because he gave you his arm to lean on? A gallant, princely gesture. Lucky he didn't pitch you over the side."

"It was polite, at least," Eilonwy remarked, "which is something Assistant Pig-Keepers sometimes aren't."

"An Assistant Pig-Keeper," Taran snapped. "Yes, that's to be my lot in life. I was born to be one, just as the Princeling of Mona was born to his rank. He's a king's son and I—I don't even know the names of my parents."

"Well," said Eilonwy, "you can't blame Rhun for being born. I mean, you could, but it wouldn't help matters. It's like kicking a rock with your bare foot."

Taran snorted. "I daresay that's his father's sword he's got on, and I daresay he's never drawn it except to frighten a rabbit. At least I've earned the right to wear mine. Yet he still calls himself a prince. Does his birth make him worthy of his rank? As worthy as Gwydion Son of Don?"

"Prince Gwydion's the greatest warrior in Prydain," Eilonwy replied. "You can't expect everyone to be like him. And it seems to me that if an Assistant Pig-Keeper does the best he can, and a prince does the best he can, there's no difference between them."

"No difference!" Taran cried angrily. "You spoke well enough of Rhun!"

"Taran of Caer Dallben," Eilonwy declared, "I really believe you're jealous. And sorry for yourself. And that's as ridiculous as— as painting your nose green!"

Taran said no more, but turned away and stared glumly at the water.

To make matters worse, the wind freshened, the sea heaved about the sides of the ship, and Taran could barely keep his footing. His head spun and he feared the vessel would capsize. Eilonwy, deathly pale, clung to the bulwark.

Gurgi wailed and howled pitifully. "Poor tender head is full of whirlings and twirlings! Gurgi does not like this ship any more. He wants to be at home!"

Prince Rhun appeared not the least distressed. He ate heartily and was in the best of spirits, while Taran huddled wretchedly in his cloak. The sea did not calm until dusk, and at nightfall Taran was grateful the vessel anchored in a calm cove. Eilonwy took out the golden sphere. In her hands it began to glow and its rays shimmered over the black water.

"I say, what's that?" cried Prince Rhun, who had clambered down from his platform.

"It's my bauble," said Eilonwy. "I always carry it with me. You never can tell when it will come in handy."

"Amazing!" exclaimed the Prince. "I've never seen anything like it in my life." He examined the golden ball carefully, but as he held it in his hand the light winked out. Rhun looked up in dismay. "I'm afraid I've broken it."

"No," Eilonwy assured him, "it's just that it doesn't work for everyone."

"Unbelievable!" said Rhun. "You must show it to my parents. I wish we had a few of those trinkets around the castle."

After a last, curious glance at the bauble, Rhun returned it to Eilonwy. Insisting that the Princess sleep in the comfort of the shed, Rhun bedded himself down amid a pile of netting. Gurgi curled up nearby, while Kaw, heedless of Taran's entreaties to leave his high perch, roosted on the mast. Rhun, falling asleep instantly, snored so piercingly that Taran, already vexed beyond endurance, stretched out on the deck as far as possible from the slumbering Prince. When Taran slept at last, he dreamed the companions had never left Caer Dallben.

About the Author

In writing the Chronicles of Prydain, Mr. Alexander says, "There was nothing to do but keep on. The story insisted on being written. . . . The people in it were born, like most children, at unlikely and inconvenient times. Gurgi, for example, appeared in the pre-dawn hours. . . . Suddenly there he was, with his groanings and moanings, looking like a disordered owl's nest." The author first met the hopelessly distraught and harassed Gwystyl while sitting, under protest, in a dentist's chair!

Lloyd Alexander was born and raised in Philadelphia. As a boy he decided that he wanted to be a writer. "If reading offered any preparation for writing, there were grounds for hope. I had been reading as long as I could remember. Shakespeare, Dickens, Mark Twain, and so many others were my dearest friends and greatest teachers. I loved all the world's mythologies; King Arthur was one of my heroes; I played with a trash-can lid for a knightly shield, and my uncle's cane for the sword Excalibur."

During World War II, Mr. Alexander trained as a member of an army combat intelligence team in Wales. This ancient, rough-hewn country with its castles, mountains, and its own beautiful language made a tremendous impression on him, but not until years later did he realize that he had been given a glimpse of another enchanted kingdom.

After the war, while attending the University of Paris, he met his future wife, Janine. They were married, and moved back to Philadelphia, where Mr. Alexander wrote novel after novel. It was seven years before his first novel at last was published. Ten years later, he tried writing for children. It was, Mr. Alexander says, "the most creative and liberating experience of my life. In books for young people, I was able to express my own deepest feelings far more than I could ever do in writing for adults."

While doing historical research for a Welsh episode in his first children's book, *Time Cat*, he discovered such riches that he decided to save them for a whole book. He delved into all sorts of volumes, from anthropology to the writings of an eighteenth-century Welsh clergyman to the *Mabinogion*, the classic collection of Welsh legends. From his readings emerged such characters as Gwydion Son of Don, Arawn Death-Lord of Annuvin, Dallben the old enchanter, and the oracular pig Hen Wen. The landscape and mood of Prydain came from Mr. Alexander's vivid recollections of the land of Wales that had so enchanted him twenty years earlier.

The five books in the Chronicles of Prydain are *The Book of Three* (an ALA Notable Book), *The Black Cauldron* (a Newbery Honor Book), *The Castle of Llyr* (an ALA Notable Book), *Taran Wanderer*, and *The High King* (winner of the 1969 Newbery Medal). He followed the chronicles in 1973 with a collection of short stories, *The Foundling and Other Tales of Prydain*.

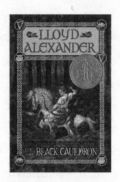